Ross stood in the doorway of the little boy's bedroom, watching as Brielle went through the motions of getting her son back to sleep. The soft soothing tone of her voice as she told Justice a story about telling the moon goodnight did little to ease the very real agitation moving through him.

An agitation he didn't understand.

Not at first.

But, as he watched the motion of her hands moving gently back and forth across the sleeping boy's back, the unease that had gripped him from the moment he'd realized she had a child began to make perfect sense.

"He's mine."

Brielle's head shot up at his low words, staring at him across the dimly lit room.

Despite the truth being all over her guilty face, he needed to hear her say the words.

"He is my son, isn't he?"

Dear Reader

Sometimes a person comes into our lives that we just can't forget, no matter how long or hard we try. For Dr Ross Lane that person is Nurse Brielle Winton. Brielle was Ross's girlfriend for several years, but when their relationship turned rocky and he was offered a prestigious internship in another state he ended things and took off for greener pastures.

But sometimes there's no leaving the past behind. Five years later Ross needs to know once and for all if Brielle is all that his memory makes her out to be and if he made a mistake in walking away.

Despite the chemistry still alive between them, apparently she isn't haunted by the past the way he is. But, having seen her again, Ross knows she is the one for him, and he's determined to win her forgiveness and give her the happily-ever-after she deserves.

I hope you enjoy Ross and Brielle's story, and the return to Bean's Creek, North Carolina. You can visit me at www.janicelynn.net or on Facebook to catch up on my latest news.

Happy reading!

Janice

THE ER'S NEWEST DAD

BY
JANICE LYNN

First published in Great Britain 2013
by Mills & Boon, an imprint of Harlequin (UK) Limited,
Large Print edition 2013
Harlequin (UK) Limited, Eton House,
18-24 Paradise Road, Richmond, Surrey TW9 1SR

ISBN: 978 0 263 23148 9

Harlequin (UK) policy is to use papers that are natural, renewable and recyclable products and made from wood grown in sustainable forests. The logging and manufacturing process conform to the legal environmental regulations of the country of origin.

Printed and bound in Great Britain
by CPI Antony Rowe, Chippenham, Wiltshire

Janice Lynn has a Masters in Nursing from Vanderbilt University, and works as a nurse practitioner in a family practice. She lives in the southern United States with her husband, their four children, their Jack Russell—appropriately named Trouble—and a lot of unnamed dust bunnies that have moved in since she started her writing career.

To find out more about Janice and her writing visit www.janicelynn.com

Recent titles by the same author:

FLIRTING WITH THE SOCIETY DOCTOR
DOCTOR'S DAMSEL IN DISTRESS
THE NURSE WHO SAVED CHRISTMAS
OFFICER, GENTLEMAN…SURGEON!
DR DI ANGELO'S BABY BOMBSHELL
PLAYBOY SURGEON, TOP-NOTCH DAD

These books are also available in eBook format from www.millsandboon.co.uk

Janice won
The National Readers' Choice Award
for her first book
THE DOCTOR'S PREGNANCY BOMBSHELL

I wrote this book while my mentor, dear friend, and the greatest doctor I've ever known battled cancer. While I was working on revisions he lost that battle. My very first Medical Romance™ was in dedication to him, because he was a real-life hero and someone I loved like a second father.

This book is in loving memory of Dr Leon Lovon Reuhland. I will miss you.

CHAPTER ONE

ROSS LANE HAD messed up big-time.

Every time his gaze settled on the petite blonde nurse in Bay Two the message reverberated louder and louder through his skull, pounding like the worst of headaches.

Idiot.

Fool.

Stupid.

Oh, yeah, he'd messed up big time five years ago.

Lately, not a day went by that he didn't wonder what his life would be like had he stuck around and been the man Brielle Winton had wanted him to be.

Funny how time changed one's perspective, one's priorities.

He leaned back against the emergency room

nurses' station, pretending to read the hospital newsletter someone had handed him moments before. In actuality, he soaked in every detail of the woman he had never been able to forget.

Beautiful as ever, she smiled at the elderly gentleman she was hooking to telemetry. Dimples dotted the corners of her lush mouth, tugging at past memories and something deep in his chest. She went about her job efficiently, smiling often, speaking in a soft, soothing tone, completely unaware that he couldn't drag his gaze from her, that tension crackled from his every pore.

She was so close.

Yet never had she felt so far away.

How could he have walked away and broken her heart?

How could he have believed that out of sight would mean out of mind?

How could he have believed she would forgive him if he showed up out of the blue five years down the road from when they'd once been inseparable and he'd stupidly thrown away what they'd shared?

She looked up, her brown gaze meeting his with an intensity that jackhammered the pounding in his head.

Her friendly smile morphed into an agitated scowl. Shooting a quick glare that told him exactly where she wanted him to go, she turned her attention back to the frail gentleman lying on the emergency room hospital bed. Her expression was immediately pleasant for her patient's benefit, her smile so potent he was shocked the man's heart monitor didn't go haywire.

Brielle had no smiles for *him*.

Not a single one.

She barely spoke to him and never when it wasn't patient related.

He didn't blame her. He couldn't. Not when almost everything that had gone wrong in their relationship had been his fault.

Almost everything, but not all.

They'd both made mistakes. His had just been bigger.

Much bigger.

Huge.

Super-sized.

Pulsating pain stabbed his temple, making him wince.

Letting Brielle go really was his biggest regret. The one thing he couldn't get over no matter how many successes he achieved, no matter how much time passed. When he closed his eyes, she was who filled his mind, who he longed to wrap his arms around and hold close, who he wanted to share those successes with.

Five years had passed since he'd touched Brielle, but he hadn't forgotten one thing. Not the sound of her laughter or the feel of her hand clasped within his. Not the way she looked upon first waking or the way that no matter how tired she'd been she'd always had a special smile just for him.

If he'd been haunted before, his memories

had escalated to torment when he'd bumped into her older brother at a medical convention. He'd known within minutes of seeing Vann that he would go to Brielle. He'd had to know if his memory played tricks on him, making the recollection of her more than the reality had ever been.

Although he had brought her up a couple of times during conversations, his former friend had barely commented on his sister, had managed to change the subject each and every time Ross had mentioned her.

Actually, Vann hadn't said much of anything about Brielle since the night he'd broken Ross's nose. That night Vann had said plenty. Lots. Mostly about how Ross had better never set foot near his sister again or he would do more than bloody his nose.

Ross hadn't fought back. He'd taken Vann's punch, figured he deserved the pain, and he'd walked away from his best friend and the woman he'd been crazy about.

The one woman who had enough of a hold

over him that once he'd learned where she was living—had Vann let that slip intentionally or on purpose?—he'd taken leave from his thriving family practice to accept a temporary emergency room position just to be near her, to work side by side with her as they once had. For the next three months he'd cover for the emergency room physician who was on maternity leave.

Then what?

Would three months be enough to finish whatever unresolved business existed between Brielle and himself?

Would three months be enough for him to know if all those years ago she had stolen his heart and he'd been too blind to realize it? Too young and stupid to know what he was losing? Or was guilt over what he'd done to her the culprit for why she haunted his dreams? Why his mind couldn't let her go?

Either way, he had to know.

He'd reached a point where he was ready to find someone to share his life with, to settle down, marry, have a few kids, and experience all the craziness that went along with being married with children.

Back in Boston, he'd been dating a beautiful, talented hospitalist, had even considered asking Gwen to marry him, but hadn't been able to bring himself to do so. Something kept holding him back.

Or someone.

So, instead of a proposal, he'd come back from his conference, broken things off with her and put his current life on hold so he could reconcile his past with his future.

The pretty little blonde, once again glaring at him from beside her patient's bed, was the starting point for him to achieve that next phase in his life.

One way or the other, his future started with Brielle Winton.

If only she'd co-operate.

Surely she needed resolution too?

Or maybe she had gotten all the resolution she

needed when he'd left. Maybe she already knew that his leaving had been the right thing and that her feelings for him hadn't been real after all. Her antagonistic attitude toward him sure gave testimony to the fact she didn't want him here.

Then again, she always had been a stubborn little thing, but that had never presented a problem before.

In the past they'd always wanted the same thing.

Almost always.

When she'd started talking marriage almost non-stop, even to the point they'd argued more often than not, he'd flown the coop.

Figuratively and literally.

He'd already been considering the internship in Boston. Not everyone got offered such a great opportunity. He'd have been a fool to turn the chance down. But he had hesitated, and he'd known why. Brielle. Part of him had resented that their relationship was holding him back, keeping him from fulfilling all his career dreams. Crazy, immature, but he'd suddenly felt a noose tightening around his neck.

Still, he regretted the panicked tailspin he'd nosedived into.

Thinking she could forgive him was pure foolishness.

Yet forgiveness was why he was here.

Brielle was why he was here, why he wouldn't leave until he had the answers he needed, why he wouldn't let her animosity get to him.

To prove his point, he winked at her, not one bit surprised when her scowl deepened.

"Dr. Lane, there's a UTI in Bay Four if you want to have a look." Cindy Whited's words interrupted his thoughts, causing him to glance at the buxomly nurse. "Her urinalysis results are in the computer for your review."

"Thanks. I'll be right there," he assured her, his attention immediately shifting back to Brielle. Their gazes collided again, causing a rumble in his chest, the same rumble he got every time he looked at her.

Love? Shame? Guilt? Regret about the past?

It was high time he knew exactly what role Brielle would play in his future. The sooner he knew, the better.

The stirring below his belt every time he looked at her left no doubt at the role he wanted her to play in his present.

His memory hadn't overplayed the reality at all. Brielle was all that he remembered and more.

He wanted her. In his life and in his bed.

She evoked his senses as no other woman ever had. Just looking at her left him wanting to drag her into the doctors' lounge and have his way with her delectable, curvy little body.

He wouldn't, of course. Bay Four was waiting. Not to mention that she would bite his head off if he tried.

Once upon a time she'd worshipped the ground he'd walked on, but that had been years ago. Now she looked at him as if she wanted to bury him six feet under the ground he walked on.

He wanted Brielle to look at him with the light

that had once shone in her eyes just for him. He wanted her to want him as much as he wanted her, for them to burn up the sheets and see if there was anything left beyond the phenomenal chemistry they'd always shared.

With the way she regarded him these days he may as well wish for the moon.

He straightened his shoulders, stared at her with renewed determination. He'd never backed away from a challenge.

Well, perhaps once, and hadn't he lived to regret that mistake?

"Forget McDreamy and McSteamy. If that man were a television doctor, he'd be McHottie." Cindy fanned her busty chest to emphasize her point.

Brielle ignored her friend's antics, as she'd grown accustomed to doing since *McHottie*'s arrival earlier that week. If only her friend knew what evils lurked beneath Ross's beautiful fa-

çade she wouldn't constantly harp on about his
royal hotness.

No, he hadn't been evil, she admitted. He'd
just… No, she wasn't going to let her mind go
to the past. Not again.

"Too bad he only has eyes for you," Cindy continued, unfazed by Brielle's lack of response.
"Because I wouldn't mind feeling the heat."

Brielle fought to keep from looking up from the
computer monitor where she was entering a patient's latest assessment data. She would not react
to Cindy's comment. She couldn't. Her friend
would have her shoved into a supply closet with
Ross and bar the door. Cindy was constantly trying to get her to date, to splurge on life's nice-
ties, as she called the opposite sex. Brielle had
other priorities.

"Take now, for instance," Cindy said with a hint
of amusement in her voice.

Brielle wasn't going to look up. She wasn't.
Ross seemed to have eyes for her a lot these days,
but she didn't care. *She didn't.*

"Here I am practically having hot flushes over those sultry blue eyes and that chiseled body, and does he even notice?" Her friend sighed dramatically. "No, he just keeps looking at you as if you're a fascinating puzzle he has to solve, as if you're a dessert he has to taste, as if—"

"You can have him," Brielle interrupted before Cindy could elaborate further, before her face could grow any hotter.

"Because?"

They'd been friends too long for Brielle not to know exactly what her friend's expression looked like without having to glance her way. Cindy's brow was arched high in question and a smile toyed on her lips.

Wasn't that the thing she'd loved most about Bean's Creek? That no one knew Ross other than Samantha and Vann? That she'd been able to move home without anyone feeling sorry for her because the man who'd been her world had abandoned her when she'd needed him most? Granted, he hadn't known the full story, but she had tried to tell him more than once and he'd refused to listen.

"He's not my type."

"Honey," her friend scoffed with another wave of her hand, "that man is every straight woman's type."

Brielle hit the "enter" key, then leaned back in her chair. "Not mine."

"Because?" Cindy persisted.

Been there, done that, have the scars and the kid to prove it.

"He just isn't."

A short silence followed and when Cindy spoke her tone was softer, more serious. "Because he reminds you of Justice's dad?"

Hello. Had Cindy read her mind? Brielle's gaze jerked up.

She shouldn't have looked. Really, she shouldn't have. Yet her gaze had instantly gone to Cindy. A very curious Cindy, who was watching her way too closely. No wonder. She probably looked like a deer caught in headlight beams. Maybe her friend really had read her mind. Or maybe she'd just thought she was talking in her head and really she'd mumbled her sarcastic remark out loud? No, she knew she hadn't.

"Why would you ask that?" Had her voice squeaked? Had the racket her mouth had emitted even been actual words or pleas to not push?

"I am your best friend," Cindy reminded her, sounding slightly offended. "Plus, I'm not blind. Dr. Lane's eyes are a fantastic blue, just like Justice's."

"Lots of people have blue eyes." She did her best to look bored with the conversation, to look as if she thought Cindy was crazy.

Cindy *was* crazy if she thought Brielle was going to have this conversation while entering patient data at the emergency room nurses' station. Especially when Ross could step up at any time.

"True." Cindy shrugged. "I just thought—"

"Quit thinking."

Cindy's brow rose, and she shook her head.

"Oh, yeah, comments like that one from my way-too-serious, too logical, always-overthinks-things friend doesn't raise questions in my mind. Not at all."

Was that how her friend saw her? Fine. She'd earned the right to be logical and serious. Brielle winced. She had to get her act together. To quit being so jumpy where Ross was concerned. Three months. Less than three months now. She could keep her cool for that long. Then he'd be gone and hopefully never come near her again.

That gave her pause.

Never see Ross again?

Not that she'd thought she ever would. Not after he'd told her he didn't want anything to do with her ever again, that she was holding him back, and he planned to get on with his life. Without her.

And he had. All too quickly he'd moved on.

Yet, here he was, back in her life, creating emotional havoc.

Just as Cindy was, waiting for an explanation.

Any moment her friend would start with the hands-on-hips foot-tapping.

"Look," Brielle said slowly, hoping to put off the interrogation, "the man annoys me and isn't someone I'd be interested in. Let's just leave it at that. Please."

Cindy considered her a moment, then shrugged. "Okay, for now, but only because your annoyance factor is about to skyrocket anyway."

Brielle took a deep breath, turned slightly to see Ross headed their way. Great. Her annoyance factor shot into orbit.

"Hey, Brielle, can I talk to you a moment?"

One one thousand. Two one thousand. Three one thousand. If she counted to infinity it wouldn't calm her Ross-ified nerves.

She could do this. She could be calm, professional. He meant nothing to her. Nothing but a pesky fly she'd like to swat away.

Swat.

"Obviously, you can."

Perhaps she shouldn't be so snappy with a physician who was her superior, but she couldn't help herself. Not so close on the heels of Cindy's question about Justice.

Her son's eyes were the exact shade of blue of Ross's. He had the same strong chin and facial structure. Made expressions that were so similar to Ross's that at times Brielle's breath caught and memories pierced her heart.

Justice looked a great deal as Ross must have looked at a similar age. Except that her son had arrived into the world two months early and was small for his age. She couldn't imagine six-foot-two-inch Ross ever having been anything but big.

"I'm going to go clean Bay One," Cindy told no one in particular as she fanned her hand over her chest one last time and grinned at Brielle while mouthing, "Hot."

When they were alone at the nurses' station, Ross sighed. "Is this how it's going to be the entire time I'm here?"

"This?" She pretended to have no clue what he referred to.

"You hating me."

"I don't hate you." She didn't, did she? She just wanted him to go away without disrupting her life further, without disrupting Justice's life. No way would she let Ross hurt their son the way he'd hurt her.

"Good to know."

"Don't let the knowledge go to your head," she advised, not wanting to encourage him in any way as keeping an emotional distance was difficult enough already. "I may not hate you, but I don't like you."

Not looking one bit nonplussed, he grinned. "Let me take you to dinner tonight so we can work on that. Once upon a time there were a lot of things you liked about me. Let me remind you."

An invisible hand jerked at Brielle's throat, choking the breath from her. No sound would come out so she shook her head.

"Why not?"

Did he really not know?

"Should I give you a thesis on the reasons? Or just the top-ten list?" she snapped, her voice freeing itself from the mute clutches of shock.

"No," he said, leaning against the nurses' station and crossing his legs at the ankles in a casual pose, too casual really. "What you should do is say yes."

"No."

"Brielle."

"Don't Brielle me, Dr. Lane. There is no reason why I should say yes. No reason why I ever would. This is a wasted conversation because there's no point to us going to dinner. Ever."

"Sure there is." There was an undercurrent to his voice that caused her head to jerk up, for her eyes to study him closely. He looked casual, relaxed, but there was a steely, determined set to his jaw.

Did he know? Had he somehow learned of Justice? Had she been wrong to believe he didn't have a clue? Really, why else would he be there?

"What reason would that be? Because I sure

can't think of a single one." It wasn't as if he'd woken up one morning and thought, Hey I miss Brielle Winton. Wonder what she's been up to. Maybe I should move hundreds of miles away for a few months so I can find out. *Right*. But, then, why else would he have chosen to work here?

Unless he'd discovered her five-year-old secret.

"Because I like you," he answered without hesitation, as if his reasons were logical and she shouldn't have had to ask.

Her heart pounded in her chest and she grabbed hold of the edge of the nurses' station, grounding herself. "You don't even know me."

"Sure I do." He sounded so self-confident, so cocky that she wanted to scream with frustration. Did he think her life had just stood still since he'd walked away? That she had been in limbo, waiting for him to come back to pick up where they'd left off?

"You may have known me better than anyone once upon a time, but not any more. Five years changes a person. I've changed."

His gaze skimmed over her, dragging slowly across each of her facial features, lower till he reached where the nurses'-station hid her body. "Not that much. You're still the same Brielle."

She fought the urge to cross her arms over her chest, her belly, her hips. "Don't act as if you know me when you don't. I have changed." Oh, how pregnancy and becoming a mother had changed her. Her body. Her mindset. Everything. Justice had changed her for the good. Unlike his father. "I'm a completely different person, have different priorities, different dreams."

He moved round the desk, stood close, quietly regarding her, seeming to consider her comment. "What do you dream now, Brielle?" His question came out soft, curious, almost a plea to know her inner desires.

As if she'd tell him anything about her dreams.

"Not so long ago all your dreams featured me," he reminded her softly, no trace of his cocky arrogance to be heard in his voice for once.

There went that jerk to her throat again, but this time she held onto her ability to speak.

"Long enough." For ever ago. "Like I said, I've changed. For however long you are here, I will treat you with professional courtesy, but I will not cater to you beyond that limited role. Anything else between us ended long ago." Five long, horrible years ago when he'd changed the course of her life by ending their relationship and moving far away. "At your bidding, I might add."

Had that been bitterness in her tone? She wanted indifference, not the slightest hint that he'd hurt her, that he still held the power to hurt her.

"Brielle—"

"Unless what you have to say is regarding a patient, please don't speak to me," she interrupted, unwilling to listen to more. "Just leave me alone."

His brows drawn together, he sighed. "If that's how you want things."

"It is." With that she turned back to her computer monitor and pretended he wasn't standing

so close, pretended that he didn't mean a thing
to her.

Not pretended. He didn't mean a thing to her.
Not really.

Not for a long time.

Not ever again.

CHAPTER TWO

GLAD HER SHIFT was almost over, a tired Brielle handed an elderly gentleman an emesis pan. "Use this if you need to throw up. Dr. Lane will be in momentarily to order something to ease the nausea." A noise caught her attention as someone entered the room. She didn't have to look to know who it was. The quickening of her pulse gave all the indication she needed. "Here he is now."

"Hello, Mr. Gardner, I'm Dr. Lane," Ross introduced himself as he washed his hands. "I've looked over your labs. The good news is that your chest pain doesn't appear to be cardiac in nature."

"The bad news?" the slightly balding, white-haired man asked, his expression pinched. His frail hands clasped the white cotton blanket covering his thin body tightly.

Brielle fought the urge to take his trembling

hand in hers while he awaited whatever news Ross had come to deliver.

"Your liver enzymes are through the roof, as are your amylase and lipase levels," Ross explained, elaborating on the details of the patient's labs and how they related to his symptoms. "I'm going to admit you to the medical floor for acute pancreatitis."

Ross spoke calmly to the man, taking time to explain the diagnosis and the medical implications. Despite the fact that she should probably go and check to see if there were any new patients to triage, Brielle found herself fascinated by Ross interacting with his patient.

She'd always known he was going to be a phenomenal doctor. He'd had such a reassuring manner about him, an aura that promised his patients everything would be okay so long as their lives were in his hands, that he'd always do his best.

When it came to his patients, perhaps that was true. In the short time he'd been at Bean's Creek, he'd certainly earned the respect of his colleagues. No one could say enough good things about the gorgeous new doctor filling in for Cassidy Jenkins.

"Brielle, will you call the medical floor and have a nurse prepare a bed for Mr. Gardner? I'll get admission orders written." He looked up from where he listened to Mr. Gardner's chest yet again. "Oh, and one more thing, go ahead and give an anti-emetic prior to his transfer, please."

He named the medication, dosage, and route he wanted it administered.

Please. No wonder all her co-workers thought he was God's gift to the emergency department. Forget the man's extraordinary good looks, which made a girl willing to overlook most flaws, but, seriously, how many doctors said please and thank you routinely? As well loved as Cassidy was, even the lovely doctor on maternity leave wasn't known for pleases and thank yous.

Brielle didn't want to like him, this older version of the man she'd once loved with all her heart. Didn't want to have positive thoughts in any way, shape, or form regarding Ross.

She didn't want to have thoughts of Ross, period.

Not good. Not bad. Not any.

Forcing him from her mind yet again, she nodded at the source of her annoyance and left the emergency room bay to carry out his orders. She'd just finished drawing up the injection when he stepped up behind her. Close. Too close.

She turned to tell him to back away, to leave her alone, but facing Ross was a mistake.

He was standing closer than she'd realized. So close that they practically touched. So close that when she looked up at him, she could see the flare of desire darkening the blue of his eyes.

She remembered that flare, that look that said he wanted her. Before he'd baled out on her, that look would have had her smiling, nodding, and them getting alone as quickly as possible.

A lump clogged her throat. She choked back a fresh wave of annoyance at how she remembered everything about him, how her body remembered every look and caress he'd ever bestowed on her. *Stupid body!*

He looked good, smelled good. It was all she could do to keep from deeply inhaling the musky scent of him. If she leaned just slightly towards him, she bet he'd feel good too. His lean body was as toned and fit as ever. Perhaps more so than when he'd been finishing his degree.

But Brielle didn't lean. Instead, she focused on the image of the last time she'd seen him when she'd gone to Boston a few months after he'd left.

An image of that wonderfully built body of his pressed against a woman Brielle hadn't known, but obviously Ross had, filled her mind. His lips had been firmly attached to the blonde stranger's. When he'd pulled back, he'd smiled at the woman, slid his arm to her lower back and whispered something in the woman's ear that had made her laugh and slap his upper arm.

Brielle hadn't laughed, but she had felt like slapping Ross. And herself for being so stupid as to think going to Boston to tell him about her pregnancy had been the right thing for her to do.

He'd told her he wanted nothing to do with her or anything that had to do with her ever again. Why hadn't she believed him?

She'd left somewhere between numb, angry, and so hurt that the airline stewardess had asked more than once if she was okay. Less than a month later she'd given birth to Justice, her obstetrician citing stress as the cause of her premature labor.

The memory of her Boston trip still held the power to almost bring her to her knees with pain, nausea, and weakness. It also gave her the power to resist the man standing before her, who was as sinfully tempting as the devil himself. Yes, she'd loved him once upon a time, but the flip side of the coin held her in its grasp much more firmly these days.

"Brielle," he began, his voice low, his eyes searching as if he knew her thoughts had gone somewhere dark. He reached for her shoulders.

"Don't!" She jerked back, clenching the medication-filled syringe between shaking fingers. "Don't you dare touch me, Ross Lane. Don't you ever touch me!"

She'd been louder than she should have been and Cindy glanced her way, frowning in confusion.

"Brielle." Her name came out as a sigh. He said something more, but the roaring in her ears prevented her from understanding his words. Had he really thought he could just show up and step back into her life? Was that what he wanted?

Who cared what he wanted?

As far as she was concerned, Cassidy couldn't come off maternity leave soon enough so that Ross could pitchfork his way back to the fiery gates that had spat him out.

She closed her eyes, squeezed them tight, hoping he would be gone when she opened them.

No such luck.

She sighed. "Please go away."

He stared at her for long moments. "Is that what you want? For me to leave and just stay gone?"

Was it?

She swallowed the lump in her throat. "The emergency room would be chaos if you left."

His lips twisted. "That wasn't what I meant, and you know it. Go to dinner with me at the end of your shift so we can talk."

"We've already been through this. I don't want anything to do with you." She fought back the bile rising up her throat. Had she purposely flung his words back at him? "What would be the point?"

"We could catch up on old times."

"Aren't you listening?" She glared up at him as if he wasn't nearly as bright as she knew him to be. "I don't want to catch up on old times with you."

He shrugged. "I'm flexible. Go to dinner with me so we can make new times."

She started to shoot him down again, but thought of Justice. This was her precious son's father. A father he'd never met. Didn't she owe it to Justice to see if Ross was man enough to do right by his son should she tell him of the miracle they'd created?

Was there really any choice a good mother could make other than to see what he had to say and then make any necessary decisions regarding her son's future?

Ross watched the play of emotions dance across Brielle's face. She'd never been good at hiding her thoughts. Time hadn't changed that.

She was considering saying yes. He wanted her to say yes. More than any sane man should, he wanted her to go to dinner with him, to spend time with him, regardless of what they were doing.

"Please, Brielle. Say yes." He didn't like pleading with her, but with their past he figured he owed her that much. Hell, he probably owed her a lot more than that, but he wasn't quite ready to grovel yet. "I want to spend time with you. Outside work."

Emotions continued to battle for dominance across her face. She didn't want to say yes. Not really. But he wasn't blind. There was still something between them, a heat, an inner connection that time, or his foolishness, hadn't eradicated.

"Let me take you to dinner. No pressure for anything more, I promise. I'll grovel if necessary."

Okay, so maybe he was ready to grovel. Groveling would be a new experience, but he'd learn to grovel with the best of them if it won him the chance of getting back in her good graces.

Her brown gaze lowered then lifted to his. "Okay, fine, I will go to dinner with you. But this means nothing, Ross. Nothing at all. I am not interested in rekindling a relationship with you or making new memories or anything of the sort. I'm focused on my future. You are part of my past that I would have preferred stayed part of my past."

Ouch. She wasn't mincing her words, but he didn't deserve any sugar-coating. Still, if she'd give him a chance he'd get there, would remind her how sweet their lovemaking had been. Sweet seemed too tame a word for what they'd shared.

As simple a thing as it was, she'd called him Ross again rather than Dr. Lane. Hearing his name on her lips pleased him way too much.

"Tonight? After your shift?" A wise man would get a commitment on a date and time. Ross was no fool.

"Tonight is as good a time as any," she sighed, her face pale as if she was battling nausea. "I want to get this over with."

Her tone made going to dinner with him sound worse than having root-canal treatment. Did she dislike him so much?

"Not that I'm not grateful you said yes, albeit with less enthusiasm than one would hope for, but why did you?"

"A glutton for punishment, obviously." She laughed a laugh he recognized as one full of irony. "But we both know you weren't going to let up until I said yes. Meet me at Julian's just down the street about thirty minutes after my shift change. A quick dinner. Nothing else."

She wasn't happy about agreeing to go but at least she'd said yes and that was a start. He'd take whatever crumbs she tossed his way until he convinced her he had seriously missed her.

Clinging to the fact that he was having dinner with her, he smiled. "You need my number in case you get stuck working late?"

"No, Dr. Lane." Deep furrows cut into her forehead with her glare. "I figured out your number a long time ago."

Brielle was late arriving to Julian's, but she didn't call or text Ross to let him know. Despite her claim, she didn't have his number, not his cellular phone number at any rate.

Sheer stubbornness had prevented her from taking it earlier when he'd offered. That and her need to put him in his place even if it had only been a short-lived balm on the mega-blows he had delivered her way.

Maybe he'd have left already.

No such luck. She paused in the entrance of the restaurant, easily spotting where he sat in a back booth. A waitress stood next to the table, her pretty face bright with interest in whatever Ross was saying, her gaze eating him up.

Some things never changed.

Not that Brielle blamed the young girl. There was no denying that he was a beautiful man. He was. Yet Ross's appeal went so much further than the deep blue of his eyes, the coal-black allure of his soft, thick hair, the strong lines of his tanned face, the width of his broad shoulders or the taper of his narrow hips. His appeal came from the sharp intelligence that quickly became apparent when in his presence, from the witty humor that was always just beneath the surface, the charm that bubbled over without him even trying, the smile that dug dimples into his cheeks and made a woman need to smile back.

Based on the waitress's high-pitched laughter and flushed cheeks, Brielle guessed Ross's charm was bubbling. Although he was probably just being friendly, the sight brought her back to when she'd gone to Boston.

Just as now, he hadn't known she was there, watching him. What had been the point? He'd told her he wanted nothing else to do with her. He'd meant his words when he'd told her he was done. Some crazy part of her had clung to the belief that he'd realize he made a mistake, that they were good together, meant to be together always and for ever. Seeing him kiss the blonde when she'd still thought of him as hers had driven his words home as perhaps nothing else could have.

She'd fled heartbroken, pregnant, and uncertain about her future.

Perhaps she should have told him about her pregnancy anyway, but she hadn't been thinking clearly, had only wanted to get far away.

Later, when her emotions had settled somewhat, she'd made the decision to take him at his word, to let him have the life he'd said he wanted and had chosen over her.

Ross had no idea he had a son.

Or did he?

Nausea hit her. Hard. The room spun. Clamminess coated her skin with hot moisture. She dropped onto a bench meant for waiting customers. Wave after wave of fear slammed into her and she thought she was going to throw up.

"Brielle? Are you okay?" Concern poured from Ross, his expression worried and his voice gentle.

She blinked at him, shocked to see him so close. Obviously he'd noticed her and had left the table to check on her. He sat on the bench next to her, his hand on her face as if checking for a fever.

"Brielle?" he repeated, but she couldn't speak, couldn't respond other than to stare at him.

Had Ross come to Bean's Creek to claim his son?

CHAPTER THREE

HIS HEART POUNDING, Ross put his hand on Brielle's forehead. Red stained her cheeks, but otherwise her face was devoid of color. Although it wasn't overly warm, dampness clung to her pale skin.

"Honey, are you all right?" He shook her shoulder lightly, trying to get her to snap out of whatever had hold of her. Not once when he'd imagined finally feeling her skin against his again had he imagined it like this.

Face pinched with pain, she shook her head in denial.

What the hell was wrong with her? Why wouldn't she look at him?

"Brielle?"

Her body trembled within his grasp, making

him want to take her into his arms and make whatever was wrong better.

Fine hairs along his neck prickled. "Talk to me. Tell me what's going on so I can help you."

She closed her eyes, swallowed then took a ragged breath.

"I need to get out of here," she mumbled, so low he barely made out what she said. "I don't feel well."

"Sir, is everything okay?" the hostess asked, the young girl's wide eyes glued to where Brielle dropped her head to between her knees.

"My friend isn't feeling well. Which unfortunately means we won't be staying." He pulled out his wallet, handed the girl a twenty. "Please give that to our waitress to cover my drink and her trouble."

His gaze went back to Brielle. She still leaned forward, rocked slightly back and forth.

"Let's go, honey." He helped her sit up, but one glance at her ashen face was more than enough to prompt him to make a quick decision.

He scooped her into his arms, waited while the hostess opened the restaurant door, and then carried her to his car, with her protesting the entire time that she could walk.

"Can you stand long enough for me to open the door?"

Still trembling, she nodded against his chest. "Put me down. I'm so embarrassed."

She felt good in his arms. What kind of cad was he anyway to notice how good she felt against him when she was ill? Still, he wanted nothing more than to keep holding her, to keep breathing in the scent that was uniquely hers. To keep feeling her warm body against his.

He'd missed her so much.

More than he'd admitted even to himself until that very moment.

"I said put me down," she said, with more gusto than he would have thought possible based on how pale she'd looked inside the restaurant. "You should never have picked me up like that!"

He didn't point out that she'd looked too weak

to stand. Now didn't seem the time to start an argument. Instead, he gently put her on her feet, keeping his hand on her, ready to steady her if she swayed, ready to sweep her back into his arms if she stumbled.

He unlocked his door, helped her into his passenger seat, then got into the driver's side of the car. Rather than start the engine, he turned to her, watched her stare straight ahead, wishing he could know what was running through her head.

"You okay?" Crazy question when she obviously wasn't, but he didn't know what else to say to break the silence stretching between them.

"Fine. Couldn't be better." Sarcasm didn't become her, but her color was beginning to look a little brighter, not so ghostly.

"What's going on? You coming down with something?"

"I'm not ill, just embarrassed at the spectacle we just made."

She attempted to make light of his question,

but he'd have to be a fool not to realize her laugh was forced.

"Nothing contagious, at any rate," she continued, still staring straight out the window.

He stared at her miserable profile, at how her shoulders sagged, at how her hand rested on her abdomen, and a possible explanation of her symptoms, of her rejection of him, hit so hard that he thought he might be ill, too.

Acid burned the back of his throat, searing him straight through.

"You're pregnant?" He hated the words, hated asking, but he had to know. Had to know if he was too late. If he'd stayed in denial of his feelings for too long, let someone else move in and steal Brielle's heart. Claim her body.

Her jaw fell. She turned to him, her eyes round and her expression aghast. "No," she denied so forcefully he couldn't doubt her. "I'm not pregnant. Why would you think that?"

"Because you were nauseated and looked like you were going to pass out." Relief washed through Ross but didn't fully ease his suspicions. "You're holding your stomach." He grimaced, wanting to hold his own nauseated stomach. "You're sure you aren't pregnant?"

Her hand fell to her side. She closed her eyes and laughed, though it sounded bitter-sweet. "I'm not pregnant."

Something about her answer struck him as odd, as not quite the whole story. "How can you be positive?"

"I'm not pregnant. Let's leave it at that." Sarcasm bit into her words.

"Maybe you are and don't know it." Why he persisted he wasn't sure. Maybe because the thought that she might be bothered him so greatly that he wanted to be one hundred per cent certain that she wasn't.

"I am not pregnant. End of story." She blew out an exasperated breath, dropped her head against his dashboard and rolled it back and forth slowly, before sitting back up to stare blankly ahead. "Men are so dense."

Wondering at her actions, he frowned. "What's that supposed to mean?"

"Just that you were oblivious when you should have…" She trailed off, closed her eyes and put her hand to her head, wincing as if in pain again.

"Headache?" he guessed, wondering why breathing suddenly felt easier at her assurance she wasn't pregnant, wondering at her comment and wishing she'd finished it.

She nodded. "I think one is coming on. If you'll take me somewhere to where I can lie down for a minute, I'm sure it'll pass."

She was looking pale again and as if she'd like to bring up anything in her stomach. "You need a bag or something to barf in?"

"Very technical term there, Dr. Lane, and, no, I don't need a barf bag. I haven't eaten anything since early this morning."

Why hadn't she eaten? Sure, they had been busy at the hospital, but she was supposed to have had a lunch-break. How had he not noticed that she hadn't taken one?

"That's probably why you feel so poorly and is likely what triggered your headache. Hypoglycemia is serious business, Brielle. You shouldn't play around with your health. You know better."

Eyes closed, face squished, she shook her head and pointed towards the road. "It's not hypoglycemia. My blood sugar is fine. I'm fine. Just drive."

Ross wasn't sure where he was supposed to take her, but a place to lie down was a requirement he didn't have a lot of choices on. He took her to the furnished apartment he'd leased for the three months he'd be in Bean's Creek.

Despite her protests that she was fine to walk, he carried her inside, laid her on his sofa, pulled her tennis shoes off and propped her feet on one of the throw pillows that had come with the apartment.

"I'll be back in just a minute," he promised. "Don't move."

Eyes closed, she grunted in acknowledgement of his comment. He fetched a glass of orange juice and a couple of tablets to knock out her pain.

"I don't recall you having issues with headaches. How often do you get these?" he asked when she'd settled back on the sofa. He placed a cold, damp cloth on her forehead and stroked loose hairs away from her face.

"Almost never." Hating that his touch felt so good, Brielle closed her eyes, willed her body not to respond to the gentle strokes of his fingers brushing over her face, her hair.

"Sometimes hormonal changes can trigger headaches."

"Stop it, Ross. I am not pregnant," she repeated, enunciating each word with emphasis.

Really, could the situation be any more ironic? When she'd been pregnant with his child, he'd failed to notice the changes to her routine, to her body. Tonight, when she'd merely felt ill, he'd immediately jumped to that conclusion. Men.

"Are you dating anyone, Brielle?"

Grateful that her eyes were closed and he

couldn't read the truth in her eyes, she held her tongue in check.

"I suppose you're not answering because you think the answer isn't any of my business. Maybe you're right that it's not. But what you do feels as if it's my business." He sighed and it sounded so weary that she opened her eyes, her gaze instantly colliding with his intense blue one.

"I want what you do to be my business, Brielle."

His admission surprised her.

"Tell me how to make that happen."

Oh, how sweetly seductive his words were to her heart and yet… "Because you're here, I'm here, and you have three months to kill?"

"I'm here because of you," he owned up, his gaze not wavering from hers. "You have to know you're why I'm here. The only reason I'm here."

She knew that. On some level she had known. Yet her heart did a jiggly dance in her chest all the same.

"I sought you out, took this job just to be near

you, and my sole purpose for being in Bean's Creek is you."

Thud. Thud. Thud. Her heart pounded against her ribs. "Why?"

"You know why."

He was wrong. She didn't know.

"Sex?" she guessed. Their chemistry seemed to zap as strongly as ever, promising just as volcanic a ride. They'd had a great sex life. A great life period, but physically they'd have won Olympic gold once upon a time. If she were honest with herself, she'd admit that she couldn't be near him without wanting to rip his clothes off, without wanting to touch him and re-familiarize herself with every aspect of his body.

"If all I wanted was sex, I wouldn't have had to leave Boston."

That she didn't doubt. Of course a gorgeous successful doctor with his looks, charm, and sex appeal would have women falling at his feet. No doubt he'd had many women during the time they'd been apart. Her heart clenched into a tight, painful ball.

"I want *you*."

"You want sex with me?"

"Not just sex." He paused, looked torn. "At least, I don't think so." He ran his fingers through his hair then squatted down next to the sofa, met her gaze with his usual confidence. "I want you, Brielle. I want you to look at me the way you used to look at me. I want you to beg me to make love to you over and over until we both collapse in exhaustion and then I want you to tell me you want me again."

Barely breathing, she shook her head. "Impossible. You can't have that. Those feelings are gone."

Yet even as she said the words the urge to beg him to do all those things drummed louder and louder through her head. Lord help her, she wanted that sweet exhaustion he spoke of, that sweet exhaustion she knew he had the power to deliver.

"Are they?" He traced his finger over her lips as if to pound home his question. "I think the attraction is as strong as ever between us."

That she couldn't deny. Just his lightest touch had her entire body tingling as if every cell had suddenly woken up after a long hibernation.

"That's just physical." Please, let it just be physical. "I'm a grown woman now and know better than acting on just physical."

Hadn't she learned that lesson? He'd been a good teacher. So why did recalling all the other things he'd taught her seem so much easier at the moment?

"There was a lot more than just physical between us."

"Was there?" she asked perversely. "I remember things differently."

His gaze settled on her mouth. His finger toyed with her lower lip, barely grazing the inner moisture of her mouth. "Tell me what you remember, Brielle. Tell me you remember how your body came alive when I kissed you, how you responded to my slightest touch." He lifted his finger to his mouth, supped off the taste of her lips. "Tell me you want me to kiss you right now because I see how your pulse is racing, how your breathing is ragged, and how your eyes are eating me up."

"I don't want you to kiss me." She closed her eyes and held her breath, but she couldn't do a thing about her crazy racing pulse. "Even if I did, all you've done is proved my point. Physical. Physical. Physical. Nothing more."

Ross laughed. A sweet, relaxed, real laugh that sounded so familiar to her aching heart that everything in her went a little haywire.

Or maybe it was the light sweep of his mouth over hers that caused everything to go haywire.

"You taste of heaven, Brielle," he whispered against her lips. "Sweet, sweet heaven."

If she tasted of heaven, then he tasted of hell.

His lips were full, sure, full of temptation, *hot*.

Every cell in her body buzzed alive as if a direct connection had been made to where his lips met hers and he'd taken control of her nerve endings and demanded they deliver ultimate pleasure.

When he pushed his tongue into her mouth, for the briefest moment she considered biting him. But what purpose would that serve? If she wanted him to stop, she'd have stopped him. Instead, she'd parted her lips, let him have his blasted way.

He was right. She wanted this kiss. Had wanted his kiss from the first moment she'd spotted him in the emergency room on his first day at Bean's Creek.

Who was she kidding?

She'd never stopped wanting him. Not from their very first kiss years ago.

It's only curiosity, she assured herself as she opened her mouth to his exploration. She just wanted to know if his kisses still set her on fire, if he still pushed her body beyond pleasure and into ecstasy.

The sensual movement of his mouth over hers assured that he did. And more.

His hands threaded into her hair. His fingers caressed her scalp, holding her to him. His touch was gentle, not forcing the embrace, allowing her the freedom to stop him if she desired. He was probably gloating that she wasn't, that she was so weak that the first time they were alone she was flat on her back, making love to him with her mouth.

Then again, one could argue that it was his mouth loving hers.

That it was his hands moving over her shoulders, down her arms, caressing her as if she were the most prized treasure.

His body that had leaned to hover just above hers.

Kissing her, he stared directly into her eyes. When his mouth lifted from hers, his breath came hard and fast against her lips. "I missed you, Brielle. So much."

She didn't answer, because what could she say? He'd been the one to leave, the one to be in the arms of another woman when she'd gone after him mere months later.

Memories of the last time she'd seen him, of his lips on the other woman's, of how quickly he'd moved on, gave her the strength to push against his chest.

"Stop," she ordered, wriggling to sit up on his sofa. "That wasn't appropriate."

He wiped his finger across his lips. Whether he was savoring their kiss or wiping it away, she wasn't sure. "You were as curious as I was. Admit it."

Curious? He had no idea.

"No."

"Not admitting to the attraction between us doesn't make it any less real," he pointed out, with way too much logic when her head was spinning.

"Doesn't matter." Why could she still feel his kiss? Taste him? She didn't want to remember. Didn't want to have new memories of him. "None of this matters. There are others involved."

His brows formed a V. "I'm not seeing anyone."

Wondering if she'd said too much, she closed her eyes. "That's not what I meant."

"There is someone in your life?"

She took a deep breath, knowing the truth was the best policy even if she'd rather not admit it. "There is."

He swore under his breath, seemed to consider his options and make a decision all in under ten seconds. His face serious, his expression pure dominant male in warrior mode, he met her gaze. "Then he is in for the fight of his life because I want what's mine."

Taken aback, she gulped. "What's yours?"

"You. You're mine, Brielle. You always have been. You always will be."

"No." She shook her head in denial. "That's where you're wrong. I'm not yours." Needing movement, distance between them, she rose from the sofa, straightened her uniform. "I haven't been from the moment you left me for Boston. Take me home."

* * *

Ross drove in silence, trying to decipher what had happened between him and Brielle. Had he taken her to his apartment in the hope of luring her into his bed?

He certainly wanted her enough that subconsciously perhaps he had hoped the evening would end with her realizing how right the chemistry between them was. Either way, he'd failed miserably. One hot, explosive kiss that had filled his head with fantasies and she'd pushed him away, demanding to be driven home.

"You wanted that kiss as much as I did."

"Do we have to talk about that again?" At his nod, she sighed as if needing lots of patience. "Fine. If your ego needs to believe that, you go right ahead and believe that I've done nothing but pine away for your kisses since you walked out."

His ego wasn't what needed to believe that she wanted his kisses. He daren't name what body part needed to believe.

Surprisingly, it wasn't the one she'd probably guess.

"What happened between us was a long time ago, Brielle. We were younger, still had a lot to learn about life. I had a lot to learn about life, about who I was and what I wanted out of a relationship. Don't you think you owe it to us to let go of your anger at me for leaving?"

"Fine."

Was that her favorite word these days or what?

"You're right. What happened between us was a long time ago, best forgotten. We'll just be professional colleagues, nothing more."

If their discussion wasn't so serious, he could laugh at that. "You and I can never be just professional colleagues. Our kiss was proof enough of that."

"That kiss was a mistake."

"Why? Because of this man you're involved with?" His fingers gripped the steering-wheel tighter at the thought of another man touching Brielle, of another man kissing her lips or holding her affections. "Whatever is between you can't be serious because no one at the hospital is aware he exists. I asked your friend Cindy if you were dating anyone. She said no. I asked Samantha, too, and she also denied that you were involved with anyone." He paused, thinking of Vann's girlfriend, whom he and Brielle had often double dated with during their heyday. "After she told me where I could go, of course."

Brielle's face pinched and she opened her mouth as if to say something then clamped her lips closed. "This is crazy. Why are you here? Why are you doing this after all this time? Just tell me and be done with it."

He didn't understand the strain to her voice. Yes, he'd ended their relationship, but it wasn't as if he'd done her wrong. He hadn't cheated or bad-mouthed her or abused her in any way that he knew of. When he'd moved out, he'd even paid the rent on their apartment for three months to give her time to find a new roommate to help with expenses.

"I told you I want you in my life," he reminded her. "I've missed you."

She clenched her hands in her lap, shook her head as if to shake his words away. "Once upon a time I'd have given anything to hear you say that."

He didn't miss her use of past tense. "But not any more?"

The skin pulled tight over her pale face. She shook her head again. "Surely you didn't believe I've spent the last five years waiting for you to grow up?"

"My growing up wasn't the issue." Wanting to expand his learning experiences hadn't been childish or immature. He'd been a man given an amazing opportunity and he'd taken it. Their relationship had been strained with her sudden desire to walk down the aisle and him knowing he wasn't ready for that, not at that point in his career and life. "I know you've gone on with your life, just as I have. That doesn't mean what is between us is finished. It's not."

After kissing her tonight, being swamped with all the old feelings but also new stronger emotions too, he was beginning to believe what was between Brielle and himself would never be finished.

"Don't bring up this man you're involved with," he warned, before she could toss that in his face. "Because you don't love him."

Twisting in her car seat to stare more fully at him, her gaze narrowed to tiny slits. "How could you possibly know that I don't love him?"

He pulled to a stop at a red traffic light then faced her, daring her to deny the truth of what he was about to say. "Because if you were in love with him you wouldn't have kissed me. Not at all and certainly not with that passion."

"You're wrong," she countered, her smile scaring him. "I love him more than I've ever loved any man, anyone. He's my whole world."

Truth echoed from each word she spoke.

Ross stared at her, unable to label the crushing sensation in his chest. Denial shot through him.

Strong denial. "No, you don't. Maybe you think you do, but you don't. You've not changed that much. You wouldn't kiss me if you were in love with another man. You aren't the type of woman to do that."

A need as potent as any as he'd ever felt hit him. A need to feel her lips against his, to reassure himself of exactly what he'd felt when he'd kissed her. No way had he imagined the emotion zapping back and forth between them when their bodies had touched.

That hadn't been just physical. He'd felt…more.

He leaned forward, intent on reminding her of those emotions, but she put her hand up, shook her head.

"Don't."

"Scared?"

"Of you?" She laughed but without any humor. "You won't hurt me, Ross. Not ever again, because I won't let you."

Was that what she thought he wanted?

"I'm not here to hurt you."

"I doubt you meant to hurt me last time either."

Her barb stuck deep. "But I did hurt you."

It wasn't really a question, but she answered anyway, her expression holding steady except for the slightest quiver of her lower lip. He hated that he'd caused the pain that lay behind that quiver.

"What do you think?"

That he'd been an idiot to leave this woman when she'd loved him with all her heart and had made him happier than he recalled being at any other time during his life.

"I loved you, Ross." Her voice was loaded with emotion. "And I believed you felt the same about me, that we would be spending the rest of our lives together. Of course it hurt when you left."

She'd loved him. His ribcage clamped down around his lungs at her heartfelt admission. He'd known she had, had heard her say the words in the past, but that had been in the past. He hadn't heard those words from her lips in five long years. She'd thought they were going to spend the rest of their lives together? She'd been ready for that then? In the midst of whatever relationship crisis they'd been going through she'd thought wedding bells would fix everything?

"Is that why you went crazy with bridal magazines and talking about getting married all the time?" he mused.

Shock dawned into realization in her golden-brown gaze. "That's why you left? Because I started talking about getting married and you had cold feet because you weren't in love with me and didn't want to marry me?"

"Regardless of how we felt about each other, we weren't ready for marriage."

"You never said you loved me," she reminded him, her voice catching. "Not a single time during the two years we were together did you ever say you loved me."

She had him there. He hadn't ever told any woman that he loved her, not even Brielle.

"They're just words. Saying labels out loud doesn't make emotions any more or less true."

But hadn't his own chest just done funny things at hearing her say the words, even in past tense?

"True." She turned to stare through the windshield, her face blank, withdrawn. When she next spoke, she sounded more defeated than he recalled ever hearing her. "The light's green. It's been a long day. I'm tired. Just drive me back to my car, please."

He did as she asked, drove them back to the restaurant in silence. He pulled into the vacant spot next to the place she'd pointed out where she'd parked her car. Funny, he hadn't even known what kind of vehicle she drove these days. When had she traded in the sporty little hatchback she'd driven for the efficient but nice four-door sedan?

He turned off the ignition, faced her, knowing he couldn't let things end where they had. "For the record, I cared more about you than any woman I've ever been involved with, Brielle."

She closed her eyes again, as if praying for patience or shielding her emotions. She toyed with the keys she'd taken out of her scrub top pocket. "That's nice, but it wasn't enough. Not then and not now. Have a nice life, Ross."

CHAPTER FOUR

ALTHOUGH PHYSICALLY, mentally, and emotionally exhausted from her workday and her ordeal with Ross, Brielle smiled at the image that greeted her when she stepped into her living room.

Toy building blocks were everywhere. In the midst of all the colorful blocks the two most important men in her life concentrated diligently on their efforts.

Justice added a block-bottomed flag to what appeared to be a bridge connecting two towering structures. He leaned back to survey his work.

"What do you think, Uncle Vann?"

The lean six-foot cardiologist, who was too serious for most of the world but who turned into a great big kid himself around his nephew, grinned and gave a thumbs-up. "Perfect touch, kiddo. Wish I'd thought of it myself."

Brielle loved her brother. A better man had never existed. How his long-time girlfriend could constantly turn down his marriage proposals, Brielle didn't begin to understand. She just hoped that whatever was holding Samantha back from grabbing hold of happily-ever-after with Vann would work out soon. Her brother deserved every happiness.

Then again, did anyone ever really get happily-ever-after outside fairy-tales?

Certainly no one in her life ever had.

"I see you two have been busy," she said softly, causing both males to glance up from where they worked on the floor.

"Mommy!" Justice's face lit up with excitement. He leapt to his feet and wrapped his tiny arms around her upper legs.

Heart swelling with joy and her eyes tearing just a little, she laughed and basked in her son's love. Soon enough he'd outgrow showering his affections on her, but for now she was the center of his world. She cherished each moment of his precious life.

She dropped to her knees and hugged her son to her, kissing the top of his shiny blond head. "I missed you today!"

She always missed him when they were apart. She loved her job, but nothing compared to the time she spent with Justice. Their son looked so much like Ross. Seeing him only reinforced how much Justice favored him. Same eyes, same mouth, same smile, same ability to twist her heart into a million pieces.

"Come look at what Uncle Vann and I made. A whole kingdom." Just as quickly as his attention had turned to her, his focus was once again on what he and his uncle had been building. He tugged on her hand and led her to where Vann sat on the floor. "This is my castle and this is Uncle Vann's. Mine's stronger and has a magic force field."

"A magic force field, eh? I didn't even know

they made magic force field building blocks," Brielle mused, checking out their handiwork.

"Obviously you've been buying your blocks at the wrong stores," Vann promptly informed her with a wink. "I did inform him that my castle has more heart."

"Just 'cos he's a heart doctor," Justice explained, eyeing his uncle's castle critically. "My castle has lotsa heart, too, plus the magic force field."

As he had been much of Brielle's life, her brother had been a godsend where Justice was concerned. Could she have survived those first few months of Justice's life, helplessly watching her tiny premature son fight for every breath, every milestone without her brother's unwavering support and love?

"Obviously," Brielle agreed, her gaze falling on the new toy packaging on her sofa. She smiled, more grateful to her brother than words could ever convey. "You'll have to let me in on the secret to knowing which packages contain the magic blocks."

Vann and Justice exchanged glances. "Think we should train her on the secret ancient methods of sensing special powers?"

Justice considered his uncle's question a moment then nodded. "She is my mom, you know."

"I know…" Vann ruffled Justice's hair "…but she's also a girl. Sometimes we guys have to stick together, you know, look out for one another when it comes to womenfolk."

"Moms aren't real girls, Uncle Vann," Justice explained with a "duh" expression, taking Brielle's hand and pointing out different aspects of their handiwork. "'Mantha isn't a real girl either. She's nice."

"Nice. Right," Vann said with a touch of sarcasm, making Brielle wonder if he and Samantha were arguing again. After fifteen years of dating, you'd think they'd have worked out the kinks by now, but perhaps some couples never worked out all the kinks.

Brielle sat down on the floor cross-legged and pulled her son into her lap, hugging his wiggling, giggling body close to her, breathing in the scent of his shampoo. Happiness filled her. Life was good. She didn't need anything more. Not a relationship with Ross or whatever he'd come to Bean's Creek to accomplish. She didn't need anything he could give her.

Not anything beyond what he'd already unknowingly given.

A big twinge twisted her heart like a dishrag.

She couldn't imagine not knowing her son, not being a part of his daily life, all the firsts, all the adventures, all the day-to-day miracles of watching him grow. Just the thought of not having experienced those things with her son made her chest ache.

Made her question long-ago decisions.

Never had she meant to keep Justice from Ross. She'd repeatedly tried to tell him once she'd realized he wasn't going to jump on board with getting married. Silly, but she'd hoped he'd take her hints and sweep her off her feet without her telling him her birth control had failed. She'd wanted him to propose because it was what he wanted, because she was the woman he wanted to spend his life with, not because they were going to be parents.

Instead, he'd balked.

Still, she'd meant to tell him, would have told him had he not kept interrupting her, telling her that they were finished and he wanted nothing more to do with her, and had she not been so devastated by what she'd seen when she'd gone to Boston to finally tell him.

She closed her eyes, breathed Justice in again, and reminded herself that she'd only given Ross exactly what he'd told her he wanted. She'd left him alone, let him live his life the way he wanted, and she hadn't interfered with his dreams.

When she opened her eyes, her gaze met her brother's. Something about how he watched her struck Brielle as odd. She couldn't quite label the expression on his face, just knew something was going on in that brilliant mind of his besides which plastic block castle was his and which one was Justice's.

Then again, they hadn't had a chance to talk about Ross's appearance. Vann had texted her the day before to tell her he'd pick Justice up from preschool so he could spend some time with his nephew and that he'd see her when she got home.

"Thanks for staying late," she told him. "Sorry I called so last minute to make sure it was okay."

"No problem. There's leftover pizza in the kitchen," her brother told her, watching her with an intensity she imagined he used while assessing his patients.

"Pizza!" Justice jumped up from her lap and grabbed hold of her hand, tugging her up. "Uncle Vann let me order whatever I wanted on our pizza. I don't like black, uh—leaves."

Brielle laughed at her son's wrinkled nose and disgusted expression.

"He ordered one with everything and one with just the things you like. Go figure."

Realizing that despite meeting Ross at Julian's

and their discussion at his place about her skipping meals, she'd actually ended up not eating a thing. Neither did she feel hungry, but she knew she needed to eat. She put a few slices on a paper plate and ate in the living room while her brother and Justice took toy bulldozers and demolished each other's castles with a lot of sound effects. They visited and laughed until Justice's bedtime. Brielle gave her son his bath, tucked him into bed with a story, lots of kisses, and a prayer. Within minutes he was sound asleep and with one last kiss to his forehead she went to find her brother.

He'd completely cleared away all traces of their building/demolition spree and now reclined, flipping through the television channels with the outstretched remote.

"Nothing's on," he commented, setting the controller on the chair arm. "He down for the night?"

Nodding, Brielle sank onto the sofa. "Thanks for clearing up the blocks, but that doesn't get you off the hook."

"You're welcome, and I didn't know I was on the hook."

"You didn't return my calls earlier this week," she reminded him, nervous energy keeping at bay the fatigue she should be feeling after her long day.

He shrugged. "You said there wasn't an emergency. I knew I'd see you today. Tell me about why you were late coming home tonight."

She eyed her brother closely. If Vann Winton was the type of man to squirm, he'd be wiggling against the leather recliner. He didn't, of course, not her big, brave older brother, but he may as well have.

"You know exactly why I was late coming home tonight, don't you? You knew he was coming." She couldn't bring herself to say Ross's name out loud.

Not bothering to pretend he didn't know exactly what and who she meant, Vann sighed. "Samantha told me as soon as she learned who was filling in for Dr. Jenkins. I can't say I was surprised."

Brielle's heart rate picked up. "Why? How could his showing up to work at the hospital where I work not be a surprise after all this time? Do you two stay in touch?"

"No." Vann's expression pinched and Brielle had another twinge of guilt, one triggered by how her relationship with Ross had affected his relationship with her brother. Vann shifted in the recliner, shrugged. "I ran into him a few weeks ago."

"Ran into him?" Panic replaced her guilt. Had Vann mentioned Justice?

"At the medical conference I spoke at in Philadelphia. He was also one of the presenters and our paths crossed a couple of times."

"That was almost two months ago," she accused, feeling as if her chest was caving in around her lungs. "Knowing what you know, you didn't bother to mention running into him?" Her heart beat wildly against her ribcage. Had Ross known all along and just been faking not knowing about their son? Had he been waiting for her to tell him?

"Why would I mention him to you?" Vann's eyes narrowed suspiciously. "You're over the man, right?"

"Right, but..." She trailed off, took a deep breath, and reminded herself to remain calm. "You know the reasons you should have mentioned seeing him to me."

His face tightened. "Justice?"

Brielle didn't answer. There was no point in answering. Not when he already knew the answer. He'd never asked if Justice was Ross's child. He hadn't had to.

"That doesn't explain why you thought he might come here."

"He asked me about you a dozen times in Philly."

Her heart quickened. "Asked what?"

"How you were, if you were married, if you were seeing anyone, if you ever mentioned him, where you lived. Those kinds of questions. He couldn't seem to get enough information about you."

Panic hit afresh. "What did you tell him?"

"I didn't tell him about Justice, if that's what you're wondering."

No, that was her job and what weighed on her mind.

"You need to tell him."

Her brother's words crashed into her thoughts.

"Why do you say that?"

Vann just stared straight into her soul, the same way he had at any point in her life when he was waiting for her to do what he considered the "right thing".

"This isn't taking a tube of lipstick back to a department store, Vann."

He didn't say a word. He didn't have to. Just as he hadn't had to when she'd gotten mixed up with the wrong crowd back in the ninth grade and had made a stupid mistake. He'd been right then. Yes, returning the make-up she'd taken had been a horribly humiliating experience, but the right action. However, this was her son's life they were talking about. Her life.

"I tried to tell him," she reminded him, hating it that her voice whined, that she sounded so defensive.

Vann didn't blink.

"He said he didn't want anything to do with me." Saying the words out loud ripped scabs off wounds best left untouched. "I tried to tell him, and he wouldn't listen."

"Maybe he wasn't ready to hear what you had to say."

Brielle's jaw dropped at her brother's calm tone. "You're defending him? Really? Why would you do that?"

Vann took a deep breath, ran his fingers through his dark hair, which was graying slightly at the temples. "All I'm saying is that maybe he's ready now to hear what you have to say. Maybe that's why he's here."

Brielle's chest swelled with—was that frustration? Anger? Hurt? "What about me? Who says I was ready to have an unplanned pregnancy thrust on me? To sit week after week in NICU, praying my premature son lived while he went off to build his career? To chase other women?"

"He didn't know about Justice, Brielle. If he had, he would have married you."

"Oh, yes, every girl's happily-ever-after dream. To know the man she loves is only with her because she got knocked up." Oh how the thought of that hurt. Like mother, like daughter. "That's so not what I wanted and you of all people should understand that."

"Don't be crude and don't compare yourself to our mother," Vann scolded, then drew his brows together in a slight scowl. "Loves? As in present tense?"

Brielle rolled her eyes. "I was speaking about in the past. Until this week I hadn't seen the man in five years."

"Yet in the few days he's been here he's put you in a major whirlwind."

"Of course he has. I'd be foolish if I wasn't upset. What if he tries to take Justice away from me?"

Vann's expression darkened. "He wouldn't do that. You're a good mother."

She stared at her brother. "Can you guarantee that? Because I'm not willing to risk losing my son to that man."

"*That man* is his father."

"Yes, but…" Oh, how she hated it when Vann made sense, when he was logical, when his voice remained calm but his words delivered thunderous blows, *when he was right*.

She collapsed back into the fluffy cushions on her sofa, closed her eyes, and faced the inevitable.

She had to tell Ross about their son.

As if the devil heard her thought and mocked the decision she'd been going back and forth on from the moment she'd first seen Ross in Bean's Creek, Brielle's doorbell rang.

When she opened the door, a distraught Ross stood on her doorstep.

CHAPTER FIVE

ROSS STARED AT Brielle's shocked expression and tried to recall what argument he'd given himself on why he had a right to follow her home, to drive around aimlessly mulling over all the things they'd said, on why he now stood on her doorstep.

"Can we talk?"

"I…" She glanced over her shoulder, as if looking at someone, then glanced back at him. "We can." She closed her eyes. "We need to." She swallowed hard. "But now isn't a good time."

Ross glanced at the expensive luxury sedan in her driveway, realization dawning. "You have a man here?"

The man? The one she claimed to love? His stomach clenched. Sweat prickled his skin.

"Yes, she does," a deep male voice answered. "What about it?"

"Vann." A myriad of emotions struck Ross. Initially, relief that Brielle hadn't gone from his arms to another man's, then overwhelming regret. This man had been his college roommate, his best friend. Why had he not fought to repair the friendship after his and Brielle's break-up? Why had he let their friendship end too? He'd lost his two best friends when he'd left North Carolina. No wonder he'd been so bone-aching miserable and lonely when he'd first arrived in Boston that he'd gone on a social whirl, trying to fill the void.

"Good to see you," he said with brute honesty.

His former friend eyed him for long moments, then surprised him by turning to Brielle.

"I've got to head to Samantha's." He bent and kissed her cheek. To Ross he only nodded then walked past him out the door.

"Don't go!" Brielle practically begged her brother. "Please, don't go."

Vann paused, turned, looked directly at her. "I figure you two have things to talk about that I'd just be a third wheel for, but…" his gaze cut to Ross and his expression hardened "…I'm only a phone call away if I'm needed."

Yeah, Ross knew exactly what Vann meant. Hurt his sister again and he'd do more than bloody his nose. That had been Vann's promise.

Brielle was staring at her brother in shock. No doubt she'd never heard the dark threat in Vann's tone before. Vann didn't do dark, but when it came to Brielle he'd hold his own with anyone.

Ross nodded his understanding at the man glaring at him.

"You don't have to go, Vann," Brielle began again, obviously not wanting her brother to leave. Did she think she needed protection from Ross?

Recalling how hot the fires burned between them, perhaps they both needed protection.

"You know I do, sis." Vann's expression seemed to be saying a lot more than his words. "You're going to be fine. Regardless, you will be fine."

Swallowing, she nodded.

"Call if you need anything. I'll be at Samantha's all weekend." He winced. "Unless we argue again."

Ross couldn't help but wonder at Vann's comment. Were he and Samantha having problems? They'd been together so long he just assumed they got along. Maybe more had changed over the past five years than just his relationship with Brielle.

He and Brielle stood on her porch, watching her brother get into his car and drive away until the taillights had disappeared down the street.

Crickets chirped in the distance. The smell of someone's barbecue floated on the night air. Ross cleared his throat.

"I suppose we could go in." She didn't sound thrilled at the prospect.

"If you don't want to, we could sit in your porch swing and talk," he offered, trying to ease her discomfort and perhaps even his own.

Her gaze went to the porch swing built for two.

He watched the emotions flash across her face, knew exactly what she was thinking. The porch swing was made for two without extra space for avoiding touching each other.

"No, come inside. We just have to keep it down because Justice is asleep."

"Justice?"

Brielle's face paled. Her mouth dropped open. She grasped the doorjamb as if to steady herself.

"I can explain," she said, but she didn't. She couldn't do more than just stare at him, her eyes filled with what? Horror? Shock? Fear?

"Who is Justice?" he asked, knowing he wasn't going to like the answer. "The man you mentioned earlier? He's here? Asleep in your house?"

She winced, shook her head. "No."

"Then who is sleeping in your house? Who is Justice?"

She swallowed. Hard. "My son."

Shock reverberated through him with the force of an earthquake.

"You have a son?" Ross was certain that it was

his eyes, his very soul that were filled with horror, shock, fear. An odd, extremely painful tug ripped at his heart. Brielle had a son. "Why didn't Vann tell me you had a kid? Why didn't you tell me?" He knew his words were accusing, but he didn't care. Brielle had a child. How could she have done that to him? The thought of her having a child felt like the ultimate betrayal. Had he really expected her to have just been waiting for him the past five years? Perhaps, arrogantly, he had. He raked his fingers through his hair then grimaced, took a deep breath. "You really have a child?"

Still gripping the doorjamb for dear life, she nodded.

"A son." He took an even deeper breath, needing oxygen in his aching lungs, needing clarity for his racing mind. "Is his father still in the picture? Is he the man you claim to love?"

"His fath— No," Brielle shook her head, not meeting his eyes. "I did love him, but he isn't in the picture. He hasn't been for some time."

Ross's brows came together in a deep V, digging almost painfully into his forehead. "Not at all? Not you or your son's?"

"He hasn't been a part of my life for a long time. Or Justice's."

Justice. Her son. That odd tug yanked at his chest again. He just couldn't believe Brielle had a child. He tried to picture her pregnant, to imagine her belly swollen with child, and he just couldn't. Curvier through her hips and breasts, her body was even better than it had been five years ago.

"Justice…" Ross said the name slowly, letting the boy's name roll off his tongue. Brielle was a mother. His Brielle. None of his fantasies of her had featured discovering that she was a mother. He didn't like the ragged emotion jagging through his mind and body. Jealousy that some man had shared that with Brielle. Red-hot, raging jealousy. She'd given birth to another man's child. Only the idiot hadn't stuck around. Disappointment that she had that strong a connection to another man, to a child who depended on her for all his needs, hit Ross in the solar plexus.

Selfishly he wanted her to himself, wanted time to explore remaining feelings between them. Instead, she really had moved on, had another life that was far beyond anything he'd imagined.

"I'm not sure what to say. I wasn't prepared for this."

"I…" She grimaced, closed her eyes then met his gaze with steely determination shining in her gaze. "Let's go inside."

Ramming his trembling fingers into his pants pockets, he followed her into the house, processing the idea of Brielle as a mother, taking in everything around him.

Unlike the apartment they'd shared, Brielle's house oozed warmth and hominess. Their apartment had been efficient and minimalist. Pictures lined these walls. Pictures of a little boy who looked remarkably like his mother with his pale hair and big eyes. They were blue rather than brown, but those eyes were so similar to Brielle's that he stopped to stare at a photo of the boy sitting in his mother's lap. Rather than facing the camera directly, they'd been looking at each other, Brielle smiling, the boy laughing up at her.

"How old is he in this one?"

Brielle paused, took a deep breath then gazed at the photo he was referring to. "He's two there."

Two. He realized he didn't even know how old Brielle's son was. "And now?"

She stared at the photo long moments, inhaled sharply. "Is there a particular reason you're here, Ross? I've had a long day."

"I wanted…" His gaze went back to the photo, stared at the boy, at the pure love and joy shining in Brielle's eyes and expression as she gazed at her son. "You're a good mother, aren't you?"

Her mouth opened then closed. Her face unreadable, she continued to look at the photo then shrugged. "I love my son. He's my whole world. I try to do what's right for him, but I'm human and make a lot of mistakes along the way."

"He's lucky to have you for a mother."

"I hope you feel that way after…" Her voice trailed off. She closed her eyes, shifted her feet, filled her chest with air then blew it out slowly.

"After…?" he prompted, instinctively knowing that whatever she'd been going to say, it had been monumental.

"Let's go and sit down."

Odd. She'd never been one to avoid conflict in the past. If anything, she'd wanted to discuss everything right then and there. Then again, there really hadn't been a lot for them to discuss. They'd rarely fought until those last few weeks.

"What changed at the end of our relationship?"

Her brow lifted. "What do you mean?"

"You were different. Why?"

"You're right. I did change." She sighed. "That's one of the things we need to talk about."

"'One of'?"

"First, tell me why you are here."

It was his turn to take that deep breath and slowly release it from his uncooperative lungs.

"Because all I could think about was you," he

admittedly truthfully, knowing tonight he had to set pride aside and be straightforward with her. "I wanted to be sure you made it home okay after you felt bad, so I followed you. I just wanted to be sure you made it okay, so I drove on past and just kept driving and driving. This evening was running through my mind and I just kept coming back to the fact that I've missed you."

"You said that earlier," she reminded him. "Why come here to say it again?"

"Because I felt like things were left wrong between us when I dropped you at your car. As if, instead of settling anything, we'd just muddied the water even more."

She flexed her fingers at her sides, curled them tightly into her fists. "You're here to clear the water?"

"I'm here because I couldn't stay away." Which was the truth, whether he wanted to admit it or not. He reached for her then stopped himself. "I want you, Brielle. The fact that you have a child doesn't change that." He raked his fingers through his hair. "Not really. Even now, I just want to take you into my arms and kiss you until you forget every man you've ever been with other than me. Until my name is the only one leaving your lips."

Brielle hadn't been prepared for this conversation. Not tonight. Sure, she'd imagined it hundreds of times in her mind, but never quite this way.

She closed her eyes, searching for the right words. Whatever words she chose, her life was going to be changed for ever. Once she told Ross about Justice their relationship would be changed for ever.

Not that she thought he'd want marriage, not now. Just as well, she'd never marry a man just because of a child.

If she'd learned nothing else from her mother's mistakes, she'd learned that lesson. Twice her mother had gotten pregnant by men who hadn't been her husband. Both times the men had married her "for the baby's sake". Both times the marriages had been dismal failures because, really, how could a marriage be a success when it wasn't based on love and knowing that person was *the one*?

Her mother, a sad, bitter, and lonely woman, had died during Brielle's senior year of high school.

"Does the turmoil on your face mean you're struggling because you want me too?" He sounded hopeful. "Tell me you want me to touch you as much as I want to touch you."

Part of her was still startled that Ross was admitting he wanted her. Then again, physical attraction wasn't enough. If it was, she'd be doing a lot more than telling him she wanted his touch. She'd be touching and kissing and dragging him into her bedroom.

Curling her fingers into her palms, she sighed, walked into her living room and sat on her sofa. "Touching isn't a good idea for a zillion reasons and that isn't what I need to talk to you about."

Joining her on the sofa, he regarded her for seconds that seemed to drag out much longer. "I could give you a zillion reasons why touching is a very good idea, but we'll do this your way. What is it you want to talk to me about?"

"Justice."

"What is it about Justice—" his face pinched as he said the name "—that you want to talk about?"

"Like I told you before, he's my whole world. I'd do anything to protect him."

He nodded. "I wouldn't expect less from you, Brielle. I've no doubt that you really are a great mother. Surely you don't think I'd do anything to interfere with your relationship with your son?"

Despite her current stress level, his praise pleased her. "No, I don't think you would interfere with my relationship with Justice." Or did she? "At least, I hope you won't." But the reality was that Ross *would* interfere with her relationship with her son. Just his very presence in their lives would shake up their whole world. "The thing is, well, Justice is—"

"Mommy?"

Both Brielle and Ross turned toward the sound as Justice padded into the living room in his superhero pajamas, well-loved stuffed frog in his hand. Why the kid had latched onto the long, skinny, stuffed frog she wasn't sure, but Ribbets was his favorite must-have sleeping companion.

"I need a drink of water," Justice continued, rubbing his sleep-swollen eyes then staring directly at Ross. "Who is that man?"

Your daddy.

The only man I've ever loved.

The man I'm trying to confess a five-year-old secret to.

"This is Dr. Ross Lane. He works at the hospital with Mommy and he's…" She searched for the right description of Ross for their son since she wouldn't be using any of her previous thoughts. "He's a friend of Uncle Vann's. They went to school together when they were in college."

"Uncle Vann is awesome," her son said with conviction, giving Ross a closer look. He wasn't used to waking up to find a strange man in their house. Curiosity and uncertainty creased his forehead.

"That he is," Ross said, seeming to finally find his tongue as he'd not spoken since Justice had interrupted their conversation.

Brielle scooped Justice up in her arms, knowing she wouldn't be able to do so for much longer as he was growing like a weed. She loved the feel of her son in her arms, of his freshly washed hair and warm little body. Her heart swelled at how much he meant to her, how much he'd blessed her life.

"Come on, Bruce," she said gently, kissing the top of his head. "Let's get you that water so you can get back to bed."

"Bruce?" Ross asked, looking confused and a bit overwhelmed. She'd felt his gaze on her and Justice while she held him, had sensed his curiosity and even awkwardness, as if he felt he was watching something private, just between them, that he shouldn't be witnessing yet couldn't bring himself to look away.

Brielle pointed to her son's superhero-covered pajamas.

"Oh, right." He laughed low, unnatural sounding almost. "Bruce."

Justice found his comment or something about it funny and began to laugh, too.

Curious about how strong, confident Ross looked and sounded awkward, Brielle hugged the giggling boy to her, kissed his brow. "Come on, giggle box. Water, then back to bed for you."

Knowing exactly how to wrap his mother around his precious little fingers, Justice put his hands on her cheeks, palms flat, and kissed her. Normally, she might have given in, held him in her lap, and just enjoyed the moment. Not tonight. Not with the past waiting to engulf her.

"That was a great kiss," she informed her son. "But you still have to go back to bed."

Frowning, Justice shook his head, his fine blond hair flying away from his head with the movement. "Uncle Vann's friend is here and I should take care of Uncle Vann's friend for him." He spoke so fast, making his argument, Brielle couldn't help but appreciate her son's sharp little mind. "He would want me to."

Fighting the squeezing motion gripping her heart, Brielle stared at her son and was curious about where his thoughts had gone. "Just how would you take care of Uncle Vann's friend?"

"I'd teach him how to build a castle like me and Uncle Vann did. You'd like that, wouldn't you?" Her son turned wide blue eyes to Ross and, just as everyone else was, Ross seemed instantly charmed by their son.

Looking directly at Justice, his face intent, he nodded. "I'm an expert castle builder. The best in the state."

Justice's eyes got huge then he shook his head, sending his hair flying again. "Nope. Uncle Vann is the best. I know he is."

Brielle's heart caught in mid-beat.

"Not biased, are you, champ?"

Justice's big blue eyes lifted to her at Ross's question.

Knowing her son didn't understand Ross's comment, she clarified. "Dr. Lane just means that you love Uncle Vann very much and sometimes when you love someone, that makes you think they are the best."

Justice, sharp as ever, seized the moment. "Like you are the best mommy ever?"

Brielle couldn't keep from kissing her son's downy head. "Exactly. Now, let's get you that water and back to bed."

Ross followed her and Justice to the kitchen, watched as she got her son's water, watched the little boy take a sip and hand the cup back to his mother with a big smile.

"Thank you," Justice said automatically, reaching for her to pick him up again. Brielle did so, letting him wrap his legs around her waist and his arms around her neck. "Love you."

"Love you, too, Bruce."

Justice giggled at her pet name for him and buried his face against her chest, yawning.

Unable to look towards Ross, she walked past him to carry her son to his bed, tucked him in, and told him a quick story while lightly scratching his back until he fell asleep.

For long moments she watched him in the low light given off from his superhero nightlight.

The safe little existence she'd made for them was about to change for ever.

Her heart beat so loudly she couldn't believe it didn't awaken her precious child.

Tonight she'd tell Justice's father that he had a son.

Ross stood in the doorway of the little boy's bedroom, watching as Brielle went through the ritual of getting her son back to sleep. The soft, soothing tone of her voice as she told Justice a story about saying goodnight to the moon did little to ease the very real agitation moving through him.

Agitation he didn't understand.

Not at first.

But as he watched the motion of her hands

moving gently back and forth across the sleeping boy's back, the unease that had gripped him from the moment he'd realized she had a child began to make perfect sense.

"He's mine."

Brielle's head shot up at his low words, staring at him across the dimly lit room.

Despite the truth written all over her guilty face, he needed to hear her say the words.

"He is my son, isn't he?"

Her hand stilled, flattened against the sleeping boy's back almost protectively. "I…" She stopped then stood slowly, taking care not to disturb Justice. "Let's go talk."

She wasn't denying it.

Brielle wasn't telling him that he was crazy, that he'd lost his mind.

She wasn't telling him that she'd met someone, gotten pregnant on the rebound, and had had that man's child.

She'd been pregnant when he'd left for Boston.

She'd given birth to his son and had never bothered to tell him.

As she walked past him to head back into the living room, he wanted to grab her shoulders, shake her, demand to know why she hadn't told him, why she would have done something so cruel. Had she hated him so much when he'd left?

She didn't look at him, just waited for him to move out of the doorway then gently pushed the door closed.

Without a word, she turned to go to the living room. He supposed it made sense to move away from the boy's room so they didn't wake him again, but he couldn't wait another second.

"Say the words, Brielle. Tell me what we both know is the truth." He spat out the demand, knowing in his soul what was coming, what seemed impossible yet blared through his being as the truth.

The truth that it seemed imperative to have confirmed verbally.

"Justice is your son." Her tone was deadpan, as if her words didn't have the effect of a tornado ripping through his mind and chest, leaving everything within him in turmoil.

She stood there, not looking at him, hands at her sides, body slightly trembling, and waited.

Ross was waiting himself.

Waiting for an explanation of why she hadn't told him about his child.

CHAPTER SIX

BRIELLE'S ENTIRE INSIDES shook. Her tongue swelled to where it stuck to the roof of her mouth. Her brain spun like a child's toy top. She felt so dizzy she thought she might fall. Her head pounded as if her eardrums had taken up a jungle beat. But she stood firm, not looking at Ross but waiting for a reaction from him.

She half expected him to turn, leave her house, and never darken her doorstep again.

Another part of her expected him to rush into Justice's room, wake him up and tell him he was his daddy.

His daddy.

Justice's father.

Tears burned her eyes, blurring her vision. Not that it mattered that she couldn't see. It didn't because she refused to look at Ross, refused to see whatever was on his face.

Her mind was doing a bang-up job of filling in the blanks anyway. Anger. Hurt. Betrayal. Disgust. Disbelief.

"You have a lot of explaining to do." His voice broke into her imaginary cocoon. He grabbed her hand. His grip didn't hurt, but he wasn't gentle either as he pulled her towards the living room, away from where their son slept.

Tension bubbled so hot she was amazed the paint didn't peel from the walls as they passed by.

"When is my son's birthday?"

His angry tone triggered a hundred old hurts, a thousand wishes of Ross being there to share Justice's birth and each year's celebration of that special day, a thousand moments of feeling so abandoned without the man she'd given her heart to without reserve. Every protective wall she had flew up.

"Perhaps if you'd stuck around you'd know the answer to that question." Sarcasm was so thick on her tongue that it left a bitter taste in her mouth, but she dug her feet in, putting a halt to their trip down the hallway. She jutted her chin and glared straight into Ross's vivid blue eyes.

Eyes that were so like her son's.

His gaze narrowed. His jaw tightened then worked back and forth once. "When was he born? How long after I left was it before my son was born?"

She told him Justice's birth date.

She watched him do the math in his head. "That's just…" His gaze grew darker, more accusing. "You knew you were pregnant when I left, didn't you?"

"He was a couple of months early." Her chin went up another notch. "But so what if I knew? What difference does that make? Either way, you left."

His jaw dropped as if he couldn't believe what she was saying. "You were pregnant with my child and didn't tell me? Don't you think that's something I had a right to know?"

Anger and hurt swelled her chest. Lifting her shoulders, she repeated words that had haunted her time and again over the years since he'd carelessly tossed them at her. "You gave up your rights when you told me you didn't want anything to do with me or anything that involved me. My son involves me. I took you at your word."

His jaw began working back and forth again, then he tugged on her arm, pulling her the rest of the way into the living room. She let him for the sole reason of hoping they didn't wake Justice.

Again without hurting her but with some force, he pushed her toward the sofa. "Sit."

With pleasure, she thought, flopping onto the sofa. Much better to sit than to end up falling on her face because of her wobbly, nervous legs.

Ross didn't sit. He stood next to the sofa, staring at her as if he were looking at a stranger. "Let me get this straight. You think my saying I wanted our relationship to end gave you the right to keep my son from me?"

I wanted our relationship to end.

Hearing him say the words sliced way too deep for five years to have passed. Maybe some blows never stopped wounding no matter how many times they'd pierced your soul.

Then again, Ross sounded pierced as well. Would he really have wanted her to tell him? To have interfered in his life?

"It's not as if I hid him, Ross." She went for flippant, but knew her attempt fell flat. "You were the one who left us."

"I didn't leave *him*," he thundered. "I didn't even know he existed."

She flinched at his harshness, at the searing truth of his claim. "Fine. You left me and he was a part of me. Same difference."

"Wrong!" As if he could no longer stand still, he paced across the room, turning and meeting her gaze. "I wouldn't have left if I'd known you were pregnant. You know I wouldn't have."

There it was. The truth she'd known and avoided so thoroughly because a man staying with her because she'd been pregnant had been the last thing she'd wanted. She'd wanted him to stay because of her, because he'd loved her and wanted her in his life for ever. She'd believed Ross had, but she'd been wrong. Never would she have trapped him into staying. She wasn't her mother.

"You think I would have let you stay if the only reason you were staying was because I was pregnant? Hardly."

"That wouldn't have been the only reason and you know it."

"I know nothing. You left so whatever the other reasons were, they weren't enough."

"I didn't know," he repeated.

"Lucky you," she seethed, going on the offensive because she didn't like being defensive, didn't like any of the feelings swirling around in her chest. "Nothing to stand in the way of your career aspirations."

"Lucky me?" He resumed his pacing, his hands thrust deep in his pockets as if he didn't know what else to do with them. Or perhaps it was to keep him from wrapping them round her neck because he looked as if he'd like to do that and more. "I've missed out on almost five years of my son's life and you call me lucky?"

When he put it like that…

"You don't even like kids," she accused, guilt punching a hole in her argument.

He stopped, turned to face her, his cheeks blotched red. "Who said I don't like kids?"

Brielle slid her hands under her thighs, feeling restless just sitting on the sofa. "I saw how you reacted earlier when I said I had a son, how you clammed up when you discovered I was a mother."

"Exactly. I discovered you were a mother." He made his claim sound like a dirty accusation. "You should have told me, Brielle. You had no right to keep that to yourself. No right whatsoever."

"I had every right." But she hadn't. Hadn't she already admitted that to herself?

"No, you didn't. He is mine. Just as much mine as yours."

Fear replaced guilt and she jumped to her feet, started pacing herself.

"What is that supposed to mean? Justice is my son." If she'd been close enough to Ross she'd have poked her finger in his face to emphasize her point. "I wanted him when you very plainly told me that you no longer wanted anything to do with me or anything that was even slightly involved with me. You told me you didn't want me in your life. Well, Justice has to do with me, is more than slightly involved with me. I carried him in my body, loved him from the moment I found out about him and more and more every day since. He is mine. You didn't want him."

"Have you not heard a word I've said? I didn't know he existed." He enunciated each word slowly, emphasizing his point.

She crossed her arms over her chest. "If you'd stuck around, you would have known."

"I shouldn't have had to stick around to know

I'd fathered a child. You should have told me the moment you discovered you were pregnant." Confusion lit his face. Sincere, real confusion. And hurt. Hurt that ran so deep he looked gutted. "Why didn't you?"

The emotional damn she'd erected to hold in over five years worth of doubt and pain burst. Tears flowed down her face and she swatted at the hot moisture. She hated this. Hated having to admit to how she'd felt when she'd discovered she was pregnant, hated it that all those same fears and insecurities were swamping her present.

"Because I loved you." She mumbled the words but couldn't manage anything clearer.

"Speak up. I couldn't understand you."

After a deep breath, she repeated herself.

He laughed. An ironic laugh, not humorous at all, that grated along her raw nerves. "You loved me? How can you say that?" He gazed at her with contempt. "You stole something from me that I can never get back."

"I…" She wrapped her arms tighter around

herself, wishing she could find a glimmer of comfort. What could she say? He was right. He couldn't ever get the time back with Justice that she'd denied him. "I didn't think you wanted to be in his life."

"A decision you made without consulting me," he pointed out, his expression terse. "You were wrong."

"I tried to tell you," she retorted defensively, reminding herself that she had attempted to tell him at their apartment and again when she'd gone to Boston.

"Right. You're a smart woman, Brielle. If you tried, I'd have known." He paced across the room, his gaze bouncing around the room, taking in every photo, every knick-knack.

Unsure what she should do, Brielle sat down again, tucking her palms up under her legs, wishing she could just snuggle down into the cushions and forget any of this had happened.

"That's what changed, wasn't it? Those last few weeks when I couldn't figure out what had happened to the amazing, wonderful woman I'd been sharing my life with? You kept acting so strange and I couldn't figure out what was different. You knew you were pregnant that whole time and, rather than tell me, you…" He stopped walking, his eyes grew round, his face reddened so much she thought he might blow his top. "That's what the sudden urge to get married was all about. Brielle, all you had to do was tell me you were pregnant and I'd have married you."

Brielle cringed. Deep and all the way through her body she cringed. "I didn't want you to marry me because I was pregnant."

"But you *were* pregnant," he pointed out, missing her point.

Bile burned her throat and she swallowed. "Pregnancy was not going to be the reason I got married. Not then. Not now. Not ever."

Ross regarded her snidely. "How'd that work out for you? You are still single? Or perhaps there's something else you need to tell me?"

His harsh question had her head jerking

towards him again. "What is that supposed to mean? You know exactly how it worked out for me. You left me. And, no, I am not married."

"I didn't leave," he corrected in a treacherous tone. "You drove me away."

She gasped, jumped back up from the sofa and glared at him. He was going to blame her for his decision to leave? Hardly. She had made mistakes, lots of them, but she hadn't wanted him to leave, far far from it. "I did no such thing."

"Sure you did. With the sudden constant tolling of wedding bells and the bridal magazines left on every flat surface in our apartment, you wouldn't stop going on about marriage and weddings. You stopped talking to me about anything but marriage and weddings and then you stopped talking to me altogether, Brielle. You were too busy being angry at me to talk to me. Say what you will, but you drove me away."

She shook her head, not willing to accept the blame. "I was trying to give you a hint."

"If you'd wanted to get married perhaps you

should have been leaving baby rattles and packs of diapers around instead of bridal magazines. I might have picked up on what you were really trying to tell me."

Acid hit the back of her throat. "I told you that I didn't want to get married because I was pregnant." She knew first hand what those marriages usually led to. An unhappy life together and eventual divorce. "I wanted to get married because I was loved."

"I did love you!"

Brielle's legs gave way and she flopped onto the sofa. She'd never heard him say those words. He never had.

She'd believed he'd loved her but never had he said them.

Until just now. In the past tense. Perhaps it would have been better to have never heard them than to feel the aching sense of loss that now swamped her. She dropped her head into her hands, feeling lost and overwhelmed.

"You never told me that," she reminded him. "Not ever."

"Like I told you earlier, I shouldn't have had to say the words." He sounded annoyed, but at least he had lowered his voice again. "Words weren't necessary. Not between us. I showed you every day how I felt about you."

"You did. You left me."

"Because you drove me away."

"Because you wanted to go to Boston. Tell me, Ross, how long before another woman was warming your bed? Because we both know it wasn't long."

"What is that supposed to mean?"

When she didn't answer he walked over to the sofa and sat down beside her, not touching her but close enough that she felt his body heat, felt the anger emanating from his every pore.

"Explain that comment, Brielle."

Hadn't she already said too much? But realistically she might as well tell him everything at this point. "I came there."

That took the wind out of his sails. "What?"

"I bought a ticket and I flew to Boston. I came to tell you about our baby, that I missed you more than I knew how to say." Her voice broke and she hated her weakness, hated how much he affected her, especially hated how much her next words hurt. "I was almost seven months pregnant and I came to tell you everything, but I saw you with another woman."

She couldn't keep the pain from her voice. She tried, but failed miserably.

"And then what? You judged me unworthy and left without telling me because I'd moved on? I dated other women, Brielle. That didn't give you the right to leave without telling me I was going to be a father."

His words hurt. Hurt deep. Deep down she'd wanted a movie moment, one of those where he cleared up what had really been happening that night, that the woman had been a long-lost cousin, that what she'd thought had looked like a romantic embrace hadn't really been anything of the sort.

"I left because when I saw you with her, I knew I'd been foolish to come there, that you'd meant what you'd said. I left because you put to rest any doubt I had about us and I had to move on with my life, too, without you."

His gaze narrowed. "I didn't have all the facts when I said what I said. You know that."

"You had enough facts that you made the decision to leave."

"I came back, Brielle. For you. I'm here right now. We've been working together this week and you've said nothing. Not a word about the fact that we have a son together." He drove his point home. "Why haven't you told me?"

"Over five years have passed since you left. I didn't know why you were here."

"You knew I didn't randomly decide to work in your hometown. I was here for you, but why I was here doesn't matter. What matters is that I was here and you didn't tell me that you'd given birth to my son. My son!" His anger rolled across the room, shaking her to her very core. "You continued to deceive me."

"I wasn't deceiving you," she said. "I never lied to you."

"Same difference. You didn't tell me the truth."

"Fine. Now you know."

"Now I know," he replied, suddenly seeming dazed. "I have a son. Justice is my son."

"*We* have a son," she corrected him, not liking his possessive tone.

His blue gaze shifted to hers, bored into her, dared her to defy him in any way. "I plan to see him, to spend time with my son."

She wasn't sure if he was talking to her or just thinking out loud, but she nodded. After how he'd reacted to learning about his connection to Justice, she'd figured that. "I have no problem with you seeing him. You can visit him here some evenings."

He shook his head. "Not good enough. I want to get to know my son. A few hours in the evenings here and there aren't going to allow me to do that. I want more. Lots more."

More? Her ribcage tightened around her lungs. "What are you saying?"

He considered her question for a few seconds then made one of those quick, confident decisions that made him the excellent emergency room doctor he was. "I'm moving in."

"Pardon?" Brielle shook her head, sure she hadn't heard him correctly.

"You heard me, and it's not up for debate."

"You're not moving in here."

"Yes, I am." He looked quite pleased with his plan, quite the arrogant, self-assured man, quite the man whose brain was making plans faster than she could thwart them. "If you don't have a spare bedroom, yours will do just fine."

"I am not having sex with you!"

His eyes were cold when they turned to her. "Oh, you don't have to worry about that any more, Brielle. Something about knowing that you kept my son from me has completely put out any flame that still burned for you."

His words stabbed deep into her chest and twisted the blade of regret painfully back and forth.

"If I stayed in your room, you could sleep on the bed, the floor, the living-room sofa." He patted the cushion for emphasis. "Or with Justice." He shrugged as if he didn't want to waste another moment even considering her. "Makes no difference because, regardless, I won't be touching you."

When she started to argue, he stopped her. "I'd suggest I sleep with Justice, but I figure it might traumatize the boy for a stranger to move into his room. Even if that stranger is his father that his mother failed to inform him of."

He meant the last to make her feel guilty again but she refused to allow him to pull that stunt with her. She'd worked hard, taken good care of her son. Ross had left on his own. He had no one to blame but himself.

"You can't just move into my house, Ross. I don't want you living here."

"This isn't about what you want. This is about what is right for Justice."

He had a point, but…

"You moving in here is right for him how?"

"He will get to know me, really know me, and I will get to know him—that is what's right. Perhaps you missed the memo, but boys need their fathers every bit as much as they need their mothers."

She couldn't argue with him. Not on that. Boys did need their fathers. Didn't Justice latch onto every second with Vann?

"There's a spare room where Vann stays sometimes. I'll clean it for you."

His haughty expression said he'd never doubted that he'd get his way, that he planned to get his way on a lot of other things too. He'd taken control of this situation and felt it within his rights to correct what he saw as major wrongs.

"Are you working tomorrow?"

She shook her head.

"I'll be by in the morning with my things." He headed to the front door. "And, Brielle?"

She met his gaze.

"Don't even think of running with my son," he warned, his voice icy. "Now that I know about Justice, I'd spend every breath I have left tracking you down, and when I found you, there would be hell to pay."

Ross paced back and forth across the living room of his leased apartment.

Nervous energy burned through him, singeing every nerve ending.

A son. He had a son. He and Brielle had a son.

An almost five-year-old son.

He'd missed nearly five years of his child's life.

He thought back to the end of their relationship, searching for some hint that she had been pregnant. Some hint that she had been trying to tell him more was going on than met the eye.

The truth was, with her erratic behavior he'd

been in a claustrophobic frame of mind and he'd probably have even missed her clues if she had set baby rattles and diapers throughout their apartment.

All he'd known had been that he'd been offered that great opportunity in Boston and he'd been torn about accepting it. Right up until he'd had enough of the bridal magazines, Brielle shutting him out, the awkwardness that had developed between them, her being mad at him more often than not, them arguing over nothing at all, and he'd called it quits.

Had he been looking for an out?

Tonight, in the heat of the moment, he'd told her he'd loved her. Words he'd never said out loud to any woman. He had cared more for Brielle than any other woman he'd ever known, but had he loved her?

He must have because the words had come from deep within him.

He had loved Brielle.

She'd deceived him in the worst way.

She'd given birth to his child and kept knowledge of that child from him.

He had an almost five-year-old son he knew nothing about.

Except that he looked like his mother and liked caped superheros.

And that the boy loved his mother.

Regardless of what he considered her wrongs, Brielle had obviously done a good job of raising their son. She was a good, loving mother, and their son adored her.

Which made things complicated.

Because Ross's gut instinct was to pursue custody, as much custody as a judge would grant him, and if that wasn't enough he'd take the case to a higher level, even if it cost him every dime he had. He would be in his son's life. But the logic that saw him through medical school and beyond warned that he had to proceed cautiously or he'd alienate his son before they ever had a chance to bond. Or traumatize him in ways therapists would warn would take him a lifetime to get over.

Ross had enough medical training to know the psychological impact his coming into his son's life could have, especially if he pulled the boy away from his mother in any shape, form, or fashion.

So he'd move in with them and Brielle would foster his relationship with Justice. Whether she wanted to or not. She owed him that much.

She owed him much more.

Once he had developed a relationship with his son, once he had all this sorted in his head about what was best for his son, then he'd decide what he was going to do about custody of his child.

Because he was going to be a part of his son's life.

An active, see-him-every-day part.

If Brielle didn't like that, it was too bad.

She'd had their son for five years, now was his turn.

CHAPTER SEVEN

THE NEXT MORNING, Brielle felt sick.

How in the world was she going to explain to Justice that Ross was moving into their house with them? Could she just say that Uncle Vann's friend was going to sleep over for a few nights and Justice not question why?

Worse, how was she going to explain to him that Ross was his father?

That one Justice would question, and big time. Rightly so.

Her son was as sharp as a tack and was going to question everything. If not immediately then very quickly as his brain started adding up the facts and coming up without answers.

She leaned forward, banged her head against the refrigerator door. Justice had woken her as usual on her days off work by climbing into bed with her and snuggling up next to her with a bright "Time to wake up!"

She'd lain there, holding him, chatting with him about whatever popped into his brain, which was a plethora of topics ranging from dinosaurs to where rain came from to where Vann's friend was. That last one she'd dodged by starting a tickle-fest because she had no idea how to tell Justice about Ross's role in their lives.

When they'd gotten out of bed, she'd been intent on maintaining her normal routine with her son, was currently in the kitchen to make breakfast for them both, but she wasn't getting much done. She kept getting distracted.

Because Ross would be there at some point.

To move in with them.

Or would he?

Why did her belly quicken at the thought that perhaps, instead of carrying through his threats of the night before, he'd high-tail it, just as he had five years ago?

To be fair, he hadn't known about their son.

As nervous as she was about the ramifications of Ross knowing about their son, she also admitted that she was glad he knew. She had never meant to keep Justice a secret from him.

She'd not told him immediately but had started hinting at marriage because in her mind she'd believed that's where they'd been heading anyway and, call her old-fashioned, but she'd wanted a proposal, a real one, not a shotgun wedding because she was "knocked up". In the end, she'd gotten neither and the longer she'd gone without telling him, the harder the thought of contacting him and telling him had become.

He'd been right. She had robbed him of something he couldn't get back. Five precious years of their son's life.

Yes, she was glad he knew.

She was also terrified.

"Mommy," Justice asked, stepping into the kitchen, fully dressed and teeth brushed, as she'd instructed him to do when she'd headed to the kitchen to start their breakfast. "Why are you head-butting the refrigerator?"

Without lifting her forehead from the refrigerator door, she turned to glance at her son, who stared at her with big, curious eyes.

"You look funny," he informed her matter-of-factly, then turned towards the doorway. "I think Mommy is knocking some sense into the refrigerator, but I don't know why. Sometimes mommies do silly things, but we kids love them anyway."

Her heart beating fast, forehead still pressed against the refrigerator, Brielle shifted her gaze to see who her son was talking to.

"Morning," Ross greeted her, looking way too handsome and relaxed compared to the restless night she'd spent. What had happened to the scowling, angry man who'd left her house only hours before?

"Having a bad day?" he asked, gesturing to the refrigerator.

She straightened, brushed her fingers through

her hair, wished she'd taken time to actually dress, brush her hair and teeth, and throw on some mascara. Instead, she wore faded old pajama bottoms sporting cartoon penguins and a cotton-candy-pink T-shirt that had seen better days but was so comfy she kept wearing it anyway. She'd twisted her hair, haphazardly clipped it back, and wore stained fuzzy white slippers on her feet.

Ross looked like he'd stepped out of the pages of a magazine advertising the perfect man. His T-shirt stretched perfectly over his chest and appeared to be of the softest cotton. His jeans fit so well they could have been custom made for his body. His hair was perfectly groomed, his eyes bright, and his smile relaxed and natural looking.

Shouldn't he look a bit harried? At least a little? Life could be so unfair.

Oh, yeah, she was having a bad day.

She forced a smile to her face. "Couldn't be better."

"Denting refrigerators a part of your new usual

morning wake-up ritual? Guess that'll take me a while to get used to."

"Or not," she countered with a glare.

Ross gave her one sharp look, glanced toward their son who watched them closely, then smiled at her. A smile that was no more real than hers had been. His served as a warning that she somehow read just as clearly as she'd read him all those years ago, back before her pregnancy and their relationship had fallen apart.

A smile that was for Justice's benefit and to let her know he expected her to mind her Ps and Qs. Their son was watching with sharp little eyes, taking in every detail of their interaction.

As contrary as she felt towards him, Ross was right.

She had to put on a positive front for Justice's benefit because how she interacted with Ross would influence how their son viewed him.

Despite her many flaws, if Ross wanted to be a part of Justice's life, she wanted that for her son's sake. She knew the statistics of children who grew up without fathers. Yes, she did her best and Justice didn't go without material needs or love and attention, but there were some things that, no matter how much she tried, she couldn't do or be for her son.

She pasted a very bright smile on her face and focused on what was most important in her life, her son. "You hungry, Bruce?"

His confused expression relaxing, Justice nodded. He climbed up on the barstool next to the kitchen counter that extended from the sink and was open on both sides of the eat-in kitchen/dining area combo room. He usually perched at the counter, coloring, drawing, or working on a jigsaw puzzle while chatting to her as she prepared their meals. Sometimes he helped.

Ignoring that Ross walked over and sat in the second barstool next to Justice, Brielle began taking items out of the fridge and setting them on the countertop.

"My daddy is hungry, too," Justice said matter-of-factly. "He's been away working for a very long time, but he's back now and he's very hungry so he needs breakfast too."

My daddy?

Brielle dropped the carton of eggs she was holding.

She'd wondered how they'd tell Justice, how they'd explain who Ross was and why he was living with them. She'd planned to talk to him about letting Justice get to know him before springing something so huge on the boy.

Obviously, Ross had taken matters into his own hands and dropped the bomb on their son.

Shaking, not wanting Justice to see her face, she stooped to clean up the eggs, paused when Ross's hand covered hers. Tumultuous emotions swirling all through her, she lifted her gaze to his. Could he see how upset she was that he'd taken the liberty of telling Justice? She hoped so. She hoped a lot of things.

"Why don't you take a morning off?" Ross's eyes darkened to a blue so deep she felt she might topple in and drown. Was that concern or mockery shining back at her? "Go and shower while Bruce and I cook breakfast for you."

Could he tell she was seething at his use of the pet name, at him having told Justice rather than allowing her to? Had he worried about what she would have said to their son or had he just arrogantly taken control without ever considering that she might have wanted to tell Justice herself?

"That's not really my name," Justice pointed out, still watching them closely enough that Brielle knew he was trying to figure out the tension in the room.

His father had been missing for the first five years of his life. Of course something wasn't right between his parents. But he wasn't quite five so he didn't understand the complexities of adult relationships. Then again, neither did she.

"I know, Justice." Ross emphasized the name, turning to look at their son for a brief moment, before returning his gaze to Brielle. "I think your mommy needs a few minutes to herself this morning. Sometimes mommies need to pull themselves together before facing their day. We guys just have to let them do their thing."

Ross remained squatting next to her, his hand covering hers and causing all kinds of electrical zig-zags and criss-crosses that annoyed her. His gaze was intent and full of…she wasn't sure. He was angry at her. Although he was pleasant, that harsh emotion was there, just beneath the surface, waiting to raise its ugly head if she didn't co-operate and do things his way. That she knew. But there was something different in his gaze, too, something more empathetic perhaps. And desire. Possibly the chemistry would always burn between them despite his claim the night before that he no longer wanted her. A claim that had hurt but which had just been another blow in an entire battlefield of injuries.

"I'm fine," she said, hoping to convince her son, if not herself. "But I do need a shower and to get dressed."

Because maybe if she wasn't in her pajamas she wouldn't feel so vulnerable.

"I'm dressed." Justice pointed to his shorts and T-shirt, then glanced at Ross and proudly announced, "I picked out my clothes myself and can tie my shoes."

"That's great," Ross praised, smiling at the boy with a raw look to his eyes that Brielle had never seen. Her heart squeezed at the monumental events happening around her.

Ross was there. Justice was there. Ross knew he was Justice's father. Justice knew Ross was his father. How many times had she imagined this moment?

"I'm pretty sure you and I can rustle up something edible that'll pass for breakfast for us all while your mom does her thing."

"I can make my own cereal," Justice announced proudly, puffing out his little chest. "I can pour my favorites without making a mess. Mommy doesn't like me eating sweet cereals too often, but she's so proud of me being a big boy and making my own."

Her son, always a talker, prattled on about his favorite breakfast cereal while Brielle could do no more than stare at Ross. He was going to make her breakfast? What, and add strychnine? Because she sure hadn't expected him to be nice to her. Was it all for Justice's sake?

"What do you think?" Ross asked, removing his hand from hers and immediately filling her with a sense of loss. "Hungry, Mommy?"

She missed his touch already.

Which was crazy.

This was not about her and Ross.

That wasn't why he was here. Whatever had been there or might have been between them had ended last night when he'd learned of Justice. Justice was their only real connection now.

She wasn't her mother.

She'd do well to remember that.

"You shouldn't call me that."

"What would you like me to call you?"

Yours.

No, she didn't want him to call her that.

Not any more. She'd just established that, hadn't she?

"You are a mommy and he's the daddy, so it's okay if he calls you that," Justice helpfully pointed out, pulling his basket of coloring books and crayons over in front of him. When he found the book he wanted, one full of his favorite caped crusader, he took out a crayon and held the box out towards Ross.

Ross Lane coloring? Brielle just couldn't picture it, but Ross took the box, selected a color and began to help Justice fill in between the lines as if he did the same thing every morning, as if he'd do whatever his son wanted of him.

Brielle stared at her son in amazement. Oh, the resilience of a four-year-old. Brielle stood, ignoring Ross's outstretched hand, and pulled out a mixing bowl.

"No."

She stopped, turned toward Ross, startled at his harsh word.

"Justice and I are going to make breakfast for you," he clarified in a more normal tone. He glanced at his son's expectant face. "Right after we finish coloring this page, right, buddy?" His blue gaze went back to Brielle. "Go, take a bath, relax, do your hair, whatever it is you women do. We'll take care of this and when you're ready, we'll eat."

Brielle hesitated.

Dared she leave Justice alone with Ross?

"We'll be fine."

That wasn't what she was worried about.

He must have read her mind because his gaze narrowed and his face darkened. "We'll still be here when you come out. I'm not like you."

He didn't have to say more. She knew what he meant. He meant that he wouldn't leave with their son and hide him away from her.

Like she'd done to him.

But that wasn't what she'd done and she wanted

to argue that point, but although Justice was busily coloring a winged car, she knew he wasn't missing a single word of the conversation. He never did. So she bit back all the things she wanted to say and smiled politely at the man who was invading her home and her life.

She'd play his game. For now.

"Fine. I'll go take a shower and be back out in about twenty minutes."

Less. Because even though she didn't really believe Ross would run with Justice, she couldn't quite get past how nervous it made her to leave her son alone with his father.

Heart slamming against his rib cage at all the morning's events, Ross glanced down at the top of his son's shiny blond head. Justice's tongue stuck out the corner of his mouth as he concentrated intently on the picture he was working on.

"You're very good at coloring," Ross offered, suddenly nervous about the prospect of being alone with Justice until Brielle returned. When he'd knocked on the front door and Justice's voice had asked who was there, he'd not been able to stop the words that had left his mouth.

Your daddy.

Without unlatching the safety chain, Justice had cracked the door, peered out at him.

"I thought you were Uncle Vann's friend?"

"I am," he'd answered. "Can I come in?"

"Mommy says I'm not supposed to let anyone into the house without her knowing."

"I'm not just anyone."

Justice's little face had twisted with thought then without a word he'd shut the door.

Ross's heart had pounded, fearful that his over-eager announcement had shocked the boy. But within seconds he'd heard the chain rattle, seen the door open.

"Since Mommy said you were Uncle Vann's friend, that makes you not a stranger, right?" Justice had asked, still blocking the door with his tiny body, as if he'd been protecting his home and was still withholding house-entering privileges.

"Right."

"Then I guess you better come in because I'm not supposed to stand with the door wide open. Lets bugs into the house. I think that's cool, Mommy doesn't." Justice's face squished up with another thought. "Are you really my daddy?"

Ross had wanted to wrap his arms around his son, to hug him close, to breathe in his scent, and never let go. Instead, he'd stepped into the house, closed the front door, and bent to one knee to put him almost at eye level with Justice.

"I am really your daddy."

Justice seemed to digest that. "Where have you been for so long?"

A thousand answers ran through Ross's mind and as much as part of him wanted to lay all the truth on his son, a more logical part of him knew that pointing fingers wouldn't do Justice any good.

"I've been working in Boston, but I'm home now and want to be a part of your life."

"Do you have to go back to Boston?"

Did he? He hadn't really made the decision that he wasn't going back to Boston, but in that moment Ross knew.

"No, Bean's Creek is my home now, here with you and your mom."

"That's cool. I've missed you."

Ross's chest tightened and he wondered how his son had missed him when he hadn't known him, but he knew what his son meant. Justice hadn't missed him but had missed having a father. Another flare of anger erupted within him at what Brielle had robbed him of, what she'd robbed their son of. How could she have done that?

"Mommy gets sad sometimes and cries at night. She thinks I don't know, but I hear her. I think she was missing you, too."

His son's words put him right back in the middle of the emotional tug of war he'd waged all night. As angry as he was at Brielle, he also admired the way she'd taken responsibility for their son, at what a good job she'd done, caring for him.

"I've missed her, too." Seeing his son's frown, he corrected himself. "I've missed you both. Very much. But I'm here now and not ever going to leave again."

Staring at the boy coloring at the kitchen counter, Ross knew he'd told his son the truth earlier when he'd made that claim. He wasn't leaving Justice, not now that he knew about him.

"I know I'm a good colorer. Mommy tells me all the time how awesome I am at staying between the lines," Justice said, so matter-of-factly that Ross laughed at the boy's nonchalance at his praise.

"Does she, now?"

Not looking up, the boy nodded. "She tells me how good I am at lots of things. Mommies are like that. It's their job."

Curious, Ross couldn't keep his next question in. "What's a daddy's job?"

That had Justice looking up at him with a

"duh" expression. "To work and take care of the mommy and the kids."

Smart kid. Ross nodded. "Yep, that's the daddy's job."

"Are you going to take care of my mommy and me now that you're my daddy?"

Justice's eyes were so intent, so eager for Ross's answer that he struggled to form words. Struggled to keep from promising him the world.

"Yeah, I'm going to take care of you and your mommy now that I'm your daddy."

What he really wanted to explain was that he had always been Justice's daddy, that he would have been there taking care of them all along had he but known about him.

He should have been there.

Brielle had been pregnant, given birth to his child.

To this adorable little boy.

Somehow he should have known, should have sensed that something monumental was happening.

His throat threatened to clog up and he cleared it just to be able to keep his lungs from collapsing from lack of air. "The first order of business on taking care of you and your mommy is for us to cook breakfast so we don't starve to death."

Justice gave him a not so sure look. "I just know how to make cereal."

"Then it's time you learn to make a good omelet. Chicks love omelets."

"Chicks?" Setting his crayon down, Justice giggled as he repeated the word.

Ross ruffled the boy's hair in what was supposed to be a light gesture. Instead, it was the first time he'd ever touched his son and his fingers lingered at the softness of his hair, at the innocence in the eyes staring up at him.

This child was his flesh and blood.

His.

Suddenly he understood the fierceness with which Brielle spoke of their son. He understood the love she felt for the boy. He felt it too, knew that he'd spend the rest of his life seeing to it that his son had a good life and knew that he was wanted, loved. By both of his parents.

As much as he wanted to take the boy into his arms and hold him close, he knew Justice wasn't ready for that, neither would he understand Ross's emotional overload. So, wishing he could somehow have the past five years to live over so he could experience every moment of this child's life, he kept the mood light by giving Justice a meaningful look. "You know, girls."

Eyes wide, Justice wrinkled his nose and went back to coloring his picture. "What do we care if they love omelets or not?"

Ross gave his son an I-can't-believe-you-said-that look. "Obviously you haven't met the right girl yet."

Justice's eyes crinkled with delight. True to the blood flowing through his little veins, Ross's son set down his crayons and regarded him with a confident expression. "I've met lots of girls. There are bunches in my preschool class." He said this as if revealing top-secret information.

"Emma Beth has a dog even." Justice's attention turned toward the items Brielle had set out on the counter. "I want a dog, but Mommy says they are a lot of work. I bet I'm good at making omelets."

Ross grinned, ruffled the boy's downy soft hair again just for another touch of his son's warmth. "I bet you are, too."

In the end, neither was good at making omelets that particular morning. Usually Ross had no problems mustering up simple dishes in the kitchen. As a long-term bachelor, he was a decent cook. But whether it was knowing that he was cooking with his son, that he was cooking for Brielle, or the constant fear that Justice was going to topple out of the chair he stood on, fall off the countertop Ross kept repositioning him on, burn himself by getting too close to the oven, or some other situation that four-year-old boys got themselves into, Ross wasn't sure. Just that his kitchen skills were lacking that day.

When Brielle stepped into the kitchen, she

was confronted by a mess the likes of which her kitchen had most likely never seen.

"Um, I see you boys have been busy." Her gaze traveled over the countertops, which were covered with various bowls, pans, and measuring utensils.

Ross just stared at her, wondering what had happened to his ability to breathe. Brielle took his breath away.

She'd changed into shorts and a T-shirt that hugged her breasts and accentuated her tiny waist. He longed to wrap his arms around that waist, to hold her to him, to see if their bodies fit together the way they once had.

So much for his claim of the night before.

Not that he hadn't meant it. At the time he had. But he'd been blinded by anger and betrayal.

Perhaps the same anger and betrayal Brielle had felt when she'd come to Boston, pregnant with his child, and seen him with another woman.

He had dated. He'd had to do something to occupy his mind, his lonely heart, because as bad as things had gotten between them, he'd missed Brielle like crazy when he'd gone north. He'd serial-dated those first few months, searching for but never finding what he'd once had with Brielle. Not ever even coming close.

"We're making omelets for chicks," Justice announced proudly, obviously not realizing what a disaster their attempt was. Then again, one had to appreciate a kid who looked on the bright side of things.

"Do what?" Her gaze jerking to Ross, Brielle frowned, obviously seeing nothing bright in the current disaster she surveyed or their son's comment.

"Uh, yeah," Ross interrupted before Justice elaborated. "Omelets for chicks. One in particular. You. Unfortunately, we ran into a few problems."

Glancing around the cluttered countertops, Brielle's brow rose. "Just a few?"

Justice surveyed their mess and wrinkled his nose. "My daddy and I aren't very good at getting chicks."

"Obviously you don't know your dad," Brielle said with the sarcasm that seemed to accompany most of what she said to or about him these days. Then, realizing what she'd said, she popped her hand over her mouth, wincing at her blunder. "Sorry," she mouthed at him, her eyes softening and holding real regret. "I didn't mean that the way…well, you know."

He did know. He'd seen his son for the first time the night before. Of course the boy didn't know him, and that was Brielle's fault.

And his own. Somewhere during the long night he'd admitted to himself that he hadn't been blameless in the events that had played out.

Rather than call her on her comment, he just shrugged as if her barb hadn't stung. "How about I take you both out for breakfast this morning?"

With one last look around the disaster they'd made of her kitchen, she accepted his olive branch. "That sounds like a good idea. On the way you can explain to me why my son has mentioned 'chicks' twice."

"Our son mentioned chicks because that's where eggs come from and we were making omelets, right?" Ross glanced at Justice for confirmation.

Being the sharp little munchkin he was, he nodded as if he were in on the biggest of secrets. He slipped his hand into Ross's and grinned. "Right."

Ross's gaze went from where his son's hand held his to Brielle's pale face. If she expected him to apologize for trying to form a bond with their son, for telling him the truth, she'd be sorely disappointed. The kitchen was another matter altogether. That he'd make up to her later by cleaning up the mess.

"Let's go before we both end up in the doghouse," he warned his son, holding onto the boy's hand loosely yet so emotionally tight that he'd never let go.

Coming to Bean's Creek had been the right thing.

Without even realizing it, he'd been coming home.

CHAPTER EIGHT

DISINFECTING HER HANDS at the nurses' station, Brielle frowned at her friend. "No, I do not want to talk about why Dr. Lane said he enjoyed the breakfast I cooked this morning."

What she wanted was to strangle Ross for saying such a thing in front of Cindy. Why did he think she insisted on taking separate vehicles to work? Was he trying to make her life as complicated as possible? Probably, as he seemed to go back and forth between being so angry at her that she could feel the almost hatred rolling off him to other softer, pleasant emotions that were too similar to the way they had once been for her liking.

"I'm not blind, you know."

"I know." Brielle sighed. "Do we have to talk about this at work, though?"

"Well, you've been busy every night this week," Cindy reminded her. She glanced towards where Ross was talking to a patient in Bay One. "Not that I haven't known why."

"It's not what you think," Brielle quickly assured her, punching a code into the medication cart.

"Oh?" Cindy's brow rose. "It's not that Dr. Lane is really your long-lost love returned from the past to sweep you off your feet?"

"Not even close."

"No?" Cindy's gaze narrowed. "Then my second guess must be the right one."

"What would that be?" Brielle asked, knowing she probably shouldn't but doing so all the same.

"That he's Justice's father and realized that he screwed up big time by not being part of that kid's life and he's here to do right by you both."

"Mostly right."

Both women jumped and spun toward Ross.

"Don't do that," Brielle hissed.

He shrugged. "What? Walk up to the two best

nurses in the hospital so I can ask one of them to get Radiology to do a chest X-ray on Mrs. Jones? Also, I'd like a comprehensive metabolic profile, a complete blood count, and a BNP to assess for congestive heart failure."

"Uh, yeah." Heat flushed Brielle's face. "I'll get right on that."

Glancing back and forth between them, Cindy shook her head. "Nope, Mrs. Jones is my patient. I've got this." Her gaze met Brielle's. "You stay and find out why my second guess is only mostly right."

Brielle and Ross watched Cindy go over to Mrs. Jones, say something to her, then draw blood from her patient's left arm.

"I should help her," Brielle said, to fill the silence that stretched between them and as an excuse to escape his always overwhelming presence.

"Scared?" He took a step closer to her, leaving only inches between them.

"Of?" She didn't budge, hating the way her feet itched to run and how his nearness affected her.

"Doing what Cindy suggested."

She lifted her chin despite how it put their faces closer together. "I'm not scared of you."

"No?"

"No." But she took off to help her friend, who didn't really need help, to the sound of Ross's laughter behind her.

The emergency department had been crazily busy in spurts and almost dead at other times. Now was one of those crazy times. Everybody available was busy but no matter how busy they were Ross was aware of where Brielle was at all times. Starting an intravenous line, giving an injection, doing an assessment, she always managed to be busy to the extent that she didn't have to spend any downtime with him.

Which should be just fine, but wasn't.

They'd been living together almost a week now and she kept him at arm's length. What was up with that? He was the one who'd been done wrong by her. He should be the one to keep distance between them. Instead…instead, he just felt confused. He'd come to Bean's Creek for her, to reconcile his unresolved emotions for Brielle. He'd not resolved a thing and was more confused than ever about the frustrating woman.

What he wasn't confused about was his son. Justice was an amazing child. Smart, funny, full of spunk. Ross was in awe of the boy's thought processes and how quickly his little mind worked. Being a constant part of Justice's life was the one certainty throughout the week's craziness. Doing what was right for his son would be his priority and if Brielle wished he'd just disappear, that was too bad.

"Dr. Lane, we have a problem." Cindy interrupted his thoughts. "Brielle just brought back a thirty-seven-week gestation female who is dilated to ten. The patient had been brought in because she was involved in a minor road traffic accident, but the shock must have sped up her labor. Brielle wanted me to get you now."

"Call Delivery and see if we can get her transferred." Ross went to the bay he'd seen Brielle go into a few minutes before while he'd been finishing up the notes on his previous patient.

"I know you want to push but try not to," Brielle encouraged the woman, propping another pillow behind her. "Is that better?"

"I have to push," the woman cried, sweat dripping down her brow. "I hurt so bad."

The woman's husband noticed Ross. "Are you the doctor? Can't you do something? She's hurting really bad. I think something's wrong because she shouldn't be hurting this bad. Is it because of the accident? It's my fault for driving too fast; I was so scared about getting here on time."

"We'll take good care of you." Ross cleaned his hands then gloved up. "I need to see how far along you are."

The woman nodded her permission, her hands

clamped tightly to the bed rail. Her husband was rubbing her arm, trying to soothe her.

"She's at ten," Brielle warned, glancing at the fetal monitor as she continued to talk. "The baby's head is crowning and another contraction is about to start."

Ross gently pulled back the covers to where he could check the woman and immediately his gaze went to Brielle's. One more big contraction and they'd be delivering a baby.

"Labor and Delivery won't have a bed available for about half an hour," Cindy informed them from where she peeked her head around the curtain.

"We don't have half an hour." Even as Ross said the words the woman's abdomen began to pull tightly with the contraction that Brielle had seen coming on the monitor.

The woman began whimpering and her husband reminded her to breathe.

"I need to push. I really need to push."

"Cindy, get some towels and everything else

I'm going to need." He glanced at Brielle, who stood at the head of the bed, keeping close tabs on the woman.

"I have to push," the woman cried. "I have to."

"Try to make it to your next contraction before pushing."

"I can't." Obviously she couldn't because she began pushing and grunting with pain.

"Breathe, honey. Don't forget to breathe."

The woman's eyes cut towards her husband and she growled something about his breathing, then she closed her eyes and cried out.

"The head's out," Ross told them as he cleared the baby's airway. "Stop pushing."

The contraction was coming to an end. The woman whimpered. Her husband moved to the end of the bed to where he could see what Ross saw. His face paled and he plopped down into the sole chair in the room.

"Put your head between your knees and breathe," Brielle told the man from where she was still attending her patient. "Don't forget to breathe."

Ross glanced up just long enough to meet her eyes and grin at her comment. She started to smile back, caught herself, and glanced away, leaving him yet again feeling as if he had been the one to wrong her rather than the other way round.

She'd denied him this. Seeing his child come into the world. Getting to be there during those first few moments of Justice's life. Being there for the first five years of his life.

"I want to push again. Please tell me I can push," the woman begged.

Ross glanced at the monitor, watched for the right time during her contraction for her pushing to be most effective. "Now. Push."

The woman bore down, pushing, crying, breathing in deep gasps.

Ross caught the baby as the shoulders appeared then the remainder of the body rushed out of the birth canal. He did a quick visual assessment of the crying baby. "Apgar is ten. Perfect. Congratulations. You have a beautiful baby girl."

Ross put the baby on the woman's stomach, clamped the umbilical cord, reached for the sterile scissors Brielle was offering him, and glanced towards the baby's father. "Do you want to cut the cord?"

The pale man shook his head. "You do it."

Ross had delivered quite a few babies during his residency, had cut the cord numerous times. But since he'd discovered he was a father, that a baby he'd help create had entered the world, he'd done neither.

Who had been in the delivery room with Brielle? Who had coached her and comforted her? Who had cut Justice's cord?

Most likely her brother had, but it should have been him. He should have been at her side, feeding her ice chips, wiping her brow, reminding her to breathe.

Justice had been two months premature. Had

his birth been a complicated one? Had he been delivered vaginally or by Cesarean section?

Had Brielle wished that he had been there or had she been grateful that he was out of her life?

Brielle watched Ross snip the umbilical cord and tried not to think about the fact that she'd just helped deliver a baby with him. Who would have believed that they'd work together to help bring a baby into the world? That she'd share the miracle of birth with him?

The miracle of birth that she'd wanted to share with him when Justice had been born.

That miracle she'd endured alone. The plan had been for Vann to be with her, but she'd gone into labor early at seven months and had needed to have an emergency Cesarean section.

Cindy came into the room with warm towels, took one and swaddled the baby in it then handed the baby girl to her mother.

"She's so precious," the woman said, obviously

still in a great deal of pain but no longer caring. "Look, she's beautiful."

The man had moved to the head of the bed and gazed down at his little girl in awe, then at his wife with more awe. "You were amazing, honey. Absolutely amazing." He bent and kissed his wife's cheek. "I love you."

Feeling as if she was intruding on a very private moment, Brielle's eyes watered and she fought sniffling. This was how it should have been.

Ross should have been at her side, holding her hand, helping her bring Justice into the world.

He shouldn't have been in Boston, living it up with some other woman, while she'd brought their son into the world alone, while she'd lain in the hospital bed watching her son be whisked away for immediate medical treatment because of his premature lungs.

All the emotions she'd felt during those moments—the loneliness, the fear, the hatred—came rushing back, making her feel weak.

She glanced toward where Ross worked, delivering the placenta. As if sensing her gaze, he glanced up, met her eyes, and seemed shocked by the animosity she aimed at him.

"You should have been there," she mouthed, unable to completely fight back the words. The new parents were so caught up in their new baby they failed to notice, but Cindy did.

"Sorry to do this, but I have to get her to the nursery for her to get a thorough once-over," Cindy said, gently taking the baby.

"Do you mind if I do that and you stay and help Dr. Lane?" Brielle asked, her eyes pleading with her friend to co-operate. She couldn't explain it, but she had to get out of this room, had to get away from Ross.

"Sure," Cindy agreed, glancing back and forth between her and Ross as if expecting to see something tangible. She wouldn't, of course. The only thing tangible between Ross and herself was the wonderful little boy who was at preschool while his parents worked.

* * *

Ross congratulated the couple once more as Cindy rolled the woman's bed out of the emergency department. Labor and Delivery had a bed available and she was being transferred for the obstetrician to examine her and to take over her care.

He glanced around the emergency department, spotting Brielle at the nurses' station, charting. He was glad that things had once again calmed down to a lull. It was only about an hour until shift change and he hoped things remained slow. Usually he did just fine, but today he felt exhausted. Perhaps not so much physically as emotionally.

Brielle's mouthed "You should have been there" had continually played through his head.

He should have been there.

He would have been there.

Had he known.

She didn't glance up as he dropped into the chair next to hers. Neither did she acknowledge him in any way. Which was an acknowledgement of its own. One that said, Go away.

"Tell me about Justice's birth."

She didn't look up, just closed her eyes and swallowed.

"Please," he added, when she didn't say anything.

"What would you like to know?"

"Everything."

"I went into labor at seven months and had to have a Cesarean section when Justice got into trouble. He was in the hospital for six weeks after his birth but other than being a little small for his age he's fully recovered."

To look at his son one would never know that he'd once fought for life.

Ross pictured what Justice must have looked like, a premature infant hooked to multiple tubes and wires, and the image gutted him. How much worse it must have been for Brielle to have lived each day with their son's life teetering on the edge. How much worse that she had to endure that alone.

"Was Vann with you?"

"He'd meant to be in the delivery room, but everything happened so fast that I delivered alone. He stayed with me afterwards, helped me keep focused on what was important—Justice. I couldn't have made it through that time without him."

"You could have, but I'm glad you didn't have to, that he was there for you."

He didn't say it was because he hadn't been there. He didn't have to. They both finished the sentence in their heads.

Brielle swallowed, then stood. "I can't do this. Not right now." She glanced around the emergency room as if searching for something to do, but there weren't any new patients and the ones currently in bays had more than sufficient nursing care already. "I…I need to go to the bathroom."

"Or anywhere I'm not," he added for her, as she rushed away from him.

Ross couldn't say coming to Bean's Creek was

a mistake. It hadn't been. But coming here, thinking that Brielle could ever forgive him, had been foolish.

Perhaps too much had happened for them to ever be able to forgive each other, but somehow for Justice's sake they had to at least try.

A week later Brielle stared across the breakfast table at a local diner where Ross and Justice sat. Much as he had since Ross had entered his life, Justice had insisted on sitting beside Ross. He couldn't seem to get enough of his father and thus far Ross hadn't seemed to mind. Actually, he seemed to soak up every morsel of Justice's attention and want more.

When Justice struggled to cut up his pancakes, Brielle automatically reached for his plate, meaning to cut them into bite-sized pieces, as she usually did.

"No, my daddy will do it."

Brielle froze, her gaze going to Ross's then lowering because she didn't want him to see how her son's words had affected her. She wasn't quite sure how to label her emotions, but for Justice's sake she just smiled and nodded.

"That's fine, Justice. Your dad can cut your pancakes for you."

For the most part she may as well not even be at the table and they wouldn't miss her. Although her son knew she was there, he was all over his new-found father. With the dogged persistence of a curious four-year-old he drilled Ross with question after question, although some of them he'd asked Ross more than a dozen times since his arrival in their lives.

Ross patiently answered each one, never seeming to tire of Justice's boundless energy and curiosity.

Where have you been?

Where's Boston?

Do you have other kids?

Brielle's heart stopped on that one. Never had she considered the possibility that Ross might have had other children along the way.

"No other kids, just you." Ross's gaze met Brielle's. "At least, no other kids that I know of."

If he expected her to crawl under the table in shame, he would be sadly disappointed. She wouldn't. She'd done the best she could given the circumstances at the time. She'd done what she'd thought had been right.

No one was perfect.

But watching Justice soak up every morsel of attention Ross gave him, Brielle had to concede that her son did need a father. Had needed one all along.

Something that she'd denied him by omission. For that, she was sorry.

"Justice, Ross can barely eat for talking. Let him finish his meal, baby, then you can ask him more questions."

Justice nodded, was quiet for almost an entire thirty seconds, staring at Ross expectantly as he took a bite then another. After three bites Ross set his fork down, probably to have a drink, but Justice started back with more questions.

"What are we going to do today?"

It was their first full day off work and preschool together since the morning Ross had moved into her house.

"What would you like to do today?" Ross countered, grinning at his son. Ross always had smiles for Justice, and patience. Had she ever allowed herself to think about what kind of father Ross would be, she'd have fallen short on the reality. Then again, all this was still new to him and perhaps he'd get bored before long.

"Mommy and I like to go fishing."

Casting a look toward her, Ross's eyes grew wide. "Fishing?"

Justice nodded.

At Ross's shock, Brielle lifted her chin. "You didn't think I was taking my son to ballet and baking classes, did you?"

"I would like to think you were keeping our son well rounded and that if he was interested in the arts or baking classes you'd be open-minded."

That surprised her. She would have taken Ross as a man's man who wouldn't want his son doing anything girly.

"What's well rounded?" Justice asked, glancing back and forth between them.

"It means you get to try a lot of different things in life."

"Like cinnamon pancakes?" Justice gestured to his plate, not something Brielle would regularly have wanted him to order as she encouraged him to eat healthily, but she'd given in to Ross's insistence that today was a special occasion. She supposed in some ways it was. Their first full family day with no work, no school, no moving into her house. Ross was there and seemingly settled in for…for how long?

No, she wouldn't think about that right now. She'd focus on Justice. His happiness and well-being was what mattered most.

"Yes, like cinnamon pancakes," she answered

her son, smiling at his cherubic face, which had a smudge of syrup on his cheek.

"And fishing?"

Brielle nodded, reaching across the table to clean the smudge with her napkin.

Clean faced, Justice turned big, imploring eyes on Brielle. "Is my daddy going to take us fishing? That's what daddies do. April from preschool said so."

To hear how quickly Justice had taken to calling Ross Daddy, to thinking of him as his daddy told Brielle how hungry her son had been for a father. That made her feel sad, as if she'd somehow not been enough.

How eager he was to spend every waking moment with Ross rather than her also made her feel a little sad.

She knew that was silly, wrong even, but she couldn't help the feeling. Even though she knew she'd done a good job raising Justice, she hadn't been enough. Not really.

Yes, part of the fascination was new-toy syndrome, but part of it was that thus far Ross had taken his role in Justice's life seriously, dedicating himself one hundred percent to the little boy when he wasn't at work. No wonder Justice was enthralled. Who wouldn't be at having all Ross's attention focused on them?

"Daddy—" the word felt so foreign on her lips, for so many reasons "—probably has other things to do."

"No, I don't," Ross quickly corrected her, eyeing her curiously and probably seeing a lot more than she wished. "My whole day is clear to spend with my family."

"We're not your family," she said automatically, without thinking. The immediate darkening of his expression told her that she'd made a mistake.

"Yes." His voice was firm, direct, offering no room for argument. "You are. Justice is my flesh and blood. My son, my family."

She clamped her mouth closed, uncertain what more to say yet wanting to say a lot, but really what could she say? He was right. Justice was as much his as he was hers and for her son's sake she foresaw a lot of tongue-biting in her future to prevent him from hearing things best left unheard by little ears.

CHAPTER NINE

WHISTLING A TUNE from a cartoon he'd watched one evening with Justice, Ross threaded line through an eye of the fishing pole he'd bought less than an hour before. He'd also bought a tackle box, lures, and a few other items he'd thought they might need to go along with the simple kiddy poles Justice and Brielle already owned and used.

Someday soon he'd buy his son a real pole and tackle, but for now the black superhero one with its emblem on the float would do. After all, the kid was only four.

"You look as if you know what you're doing, but do you actually know how to fish?" Brielle asked from where she was perched on a rock, watching him rather than baiting her hook. Then again, she'd already informed him that they usually used plastic bait rather than live crickets or earthworms.

What was the fun in that for a little boy?

He'd bought both, but after a few minutes of watching the crickets and letting the earthworms crawl around in his palm, Justice had lost interest. Right now he was stooped over just out of earshot, more interested in searching through the rocks, looking for dinosaur fossils, than in fishing. Apparently dinosaurs were starting to give Justice's favorite superhero a run for his billions.

"I grew up just a few hours away, Brielle. Of course I know how to fish. My dad and I went fishing several times a month during school breaks. Those times are some of my favorite memories of my childhood. The last time he and my mom came up to Boston we chartered a boat and went out for a day of fishing." He smiled at the memory. "It was a good day."

A slight frown marred her forehead. "How come I never knew that about you?"

Not sure how to answer her question, he

shrugged. "You never asked. When I was with you I had other things on my mind besides fishing."

When he and Brielle had been together, she'd occupied way too many of his thoughts. Ultimately, when their relationship had become stressed, he'd resented the distraction. Obviously, out of sight was not out of mind when it had come to Brielle Winton, though. Far far from it. He'd never forgotten her, never gotten over her. Now that he knew she was the mother of his child he accepted that she was part of his life. For ever. Even with how strained their relationship currently was, he couldn't say he resented her effect on him. Not this time. He was older, wiser, had learned a lot of life lessons.

"*We* never went fishing," she pointed out, almost sounding accusatory, and he grinned at the near pouty expression on her pretty face.

"I was in medical school and pouring my heart and soul into becoming the best doctor I could be," he reminded her. "What little free time I had to spend with you, well, I didn't want to spend that time fishing."

She blushed bright red and Ross bit back a smile. If she recalled, she wouldn't have wanted to spend their limited free time fishing either, unless it had been fishing in the dark for each other.

"No, I guess we didn't have a lot of spare time for things like fishing…" Her voice trailed off, then she lifted needy eyes to him. "We did have a lot of good times, didn't we, Ross? I didn't imagine that, did I?"

He tied the line around the hook, knotted it, then secured it to the pole by looping the tip around an eye. He stood the pole next to him, propping it against the tackle box and holding it loosely in his grip just to have something to do with his hand.

"We had a lot of good times together." He looked at her, at the nostalgic expression on her face, and he mentally kicked himself yet again. How could he have tossed away their relationship without fighting for her? Without trying to correct the things that had gone wrong? He knew the answers, of course, but he couldn't help but think that if he had his life to live over from that point, he wouldn't have left Brielle behind. He'd have convinced her to go with him, have put effort into repairing their relationship. And that was even without the knowledge that she'd been pregnant. "You know we did."

Memories of chasing her around their apartment, both of them laughing so hard they could barely breathe, of catching her and tickling her while she squirmed, trying to escape, of his touches soon going from playful torture to sexually charged. Of her lips going from teasing to moaning with pleasure. Of her squirming morphing into needy gyrations as his body took control of hers.

But not just the sex. Memories of holding her while she'd cried after her first code where the patient had died, letting her fall asleep in his arms, and lying there breathing her in, feeling as if she had been right where she'd belonged, feeling as if he'd been right where he'd belonged.

With Brielle.

That same feeling hit him, making him grip the fishing pole tighter. For the first time in five years he was where he belonged. With Brielle.

"Great times," Ross rasped, then cleared his throat, hoping to ease the tightness clamping down on his vocal cords. "We were great. The best."

His gaze met Brielle's and the tightness took hold of his whole body. He'd often heard the expression "tension so thick you could cut it with a knife." This was one of those moments. A moment so intense that emotions were almost palpable around them. Sexual tension. Physical tension. Emotional tension. Mental tension. Tensions he couldn't label pulsed between them.

The past. The present. The future.

All pulsated alive and real between them.

Her chest rose and fell in rapid, shallow breaths. Her lips parted.

He fought kissing her. He wanted to kiss her, to hold her, to chase her around until they collapsed together in laughter and kisses. And more. He wanted so much more with this woman.

If Justice wasn't a few yards away, he would kiss her.

He missed kissing her. Missed the feel of her plump lips pressed to his, the feel of her warm breath against his mouth, the taste of her sweetness.

They had been great together, the best.

No other woman even compared to the one sitting a few feet from him, staring at him with a hundred emotions shining in her eyes, not the least of which was desire matching his own.

And anger that was just as strong as his. She roller-coastered back and forth between the positive and negative between them, just as he had for the past two weeks.

He'd come to Bean's Creek for her, to rekindle any sparks that remained between them. The reality was that wildfire burned any time they were near each other. Then he'd discovered she'd had his child.

A child she'd kept from him and would have continued to keep from him had he not come looking for her.

He could so easily hate her for depriving him of his son. Just as she could so easily hate him for not being there for her during her pregnancy, during her delivery, during all the days, weeks, months, and years that had followed while she'd cared for their son alone.

"They were great times." Brielle finally spoke from her perch on the small boulder. She pulled her knees up close to her body, wrapped her arms around her bare legs. "Then you left so perhaps they weren't so great after all or you would have stayed."

He was the one who was supposed to be angry, not her. He was the one who had been cheated out of five years of his precious son's life. She had done that to him.

So why did her softly spoken words gut him?

Make him want to beg for forgiveness for leaving her when she'd needed him? For letting her give birth to their son alone when he should have been at her side? Ever since they'd shared the delivery earlier that week, he'd been haunted by the image of her bringing their son into the world alone. Yes, he blamed her, but he also blamed himself. A lot.

He should have been there, should have helped ease her financial burden, her physical and emotional load as she'd struggled with the trauma of a premature baby who had required weeks of hospital care. How had she managed the medical bills? Had Vann lightened her load? Not that she seemed to mind raising their child by herself, otherwise she would have asked for child support.

If only she had.

He'd been such a fool to leave her, but perhaps if he'd stayed his resentment would have festered. He'd like to think not, but he'd been immature in some ways, had had a lot of growing up to do.

He wasn't the same man who'd left her. Not by a long stretch.

He glanced at where she hugged her legs. From his position he had a perfect view up her shorts leg to see the hint of the curvature of her creamy thigh. Nothing more, just a glimpse up her shorts, a cheap thrill really, but that was all it took to make him want to push her back on that rock and rediscover her body, to search out and cherish the changes carrying their son had added to it, knowing that those changes were honored badges of her motherhood.

Noticing his gaze, she glanced down, tugged on her shorts. "Sorry."

"Brielle, I…" He paused, trying to figure out what it was he wanted to say to this complex woman who held so much power over him. Did she even realize? "I wasn't telling the truth last week when I said I could sleep in the same bed with you without wanting to touch you. This week has been strained with us in the same house, but, no matter how upset or angry I am with you, I can't be within ten feet of you without wanting to touch you."

She tugged on her shorts again, as if she was trying to stretch them over every piece of exposed skin to keep his prying eyes away.

"Why are you telling me this? I don't want you to touch me." But she was lying and they both knew it. He could see the truth in her eyes. In the way her nipples puckered through her bra and T-shirt to declare just how much he affected her, just how much she wanted to be touched.

"But it's not just the wanting that is between us," he continued. "You make me feel more than any other person I've ever known. In a single minute you can take me through every emotion. No one else can do that. Just you."

She quit tugging on her shorts, stared at him as if trying to decide if he was serious or if he was setting her up some way just so he could knock her down. He hated the mistrust with which she gazed at him, but he supposed only time would heal some wounds.

"You think you don't affect me just as strongly?" she asked, adjusting her gaze to stare out at the sparkles from the sun on the lake water. "I don't want you here and yet…" Her voice trailed off and she shrugged.

"You don't want me to leave?"

She turned, smiled softly, sadly. "No, Ross, I don't want you to go. I never wanted you to leave. Despite what you may believe, I always wanted you in Justice's life." When he started to speak, she lifted her hand to stop him. "Maybe you find that hard to believe since I didn't tell you. All I can say is that I did want you there and I missed that you weren't there. Always. More than you will ever know or believe. Let's leave it at that, okay?"

He didn't want to leave anything. He wanted her to explain, to make him understand how she'd made the decisions she had and had thought they had been the right decisions when they had meant keeping his son from him. But at the moment he

wanted to have a truce with her more than anything else.

"For Justice's sake," he said, knowing that at
some point they would have to discuss the very
things she'd just asked him to leave alone.

"And although we both feel this heat between
us, Ross, we have to ignore it," she continued,
her gaze going to where their son was studying
a rock he held in his palm. "Justice wouldn't understand."

Did she think he was going to do her up against
the kitchen counters with their son around?
Hardly.

"If we opted to become sexually involved with
each other again," Ross began, "he wouldn't have
to know. Neither should he know, really."

Shaking her head, she laughed at his comment.
"You'll quickly learn that there is no keeping
things from Justice. He'd know something was
happening between us. Just as he knows there
are negative feelings between us regardless of
the fact we pretend otherwise in front of him."

On that she was right and he agreed one hundred percent. Justice might be just under five and Ross had just met him, but he could tell the boy was very perceptive.

He glanced at their son, watched the boy intently examining the rock. That was his child, his flesh and blood. Amazing how quickly the boy had stolen his heart. Then again, Justice was also half Brielle.

He took a deep breath, blew it out, and felt a great deal of tension leave his body along with the air. "Which is why, despite how betrayed I feel by the choices you made five years ago and every day since, I am going to let that hurt go and move forward, because from this point on we have to focus on the future, on what is right for our son."

"I… Yes, you're right." Brielle nodded in agreement. "I agree. Justice is what's most important. His well-being. Thank you for understanding that."

He understood much more than she gave him

credit for. He wondered just how agreeable she was going to be when he pressed forward. Probably not nearly so accommodating as her current smiling face.

"On that same token," he told her, watching her closely, "you have to let go that I left, Brielle."

Her amicable expression paled.

"You can't keep bringing it up," he continued, determined to see this through. Not only for Justice but for both their sakes, too. They needed peace, for the past to be in the past, for the present to be clear so they could figure out the future. "You can't keep throwing the past between us as a barrier to us starting over and forging a new relationship, whatever that relationship might be."

Her eyes widened.

"It's time you forgave me." Past time as far as he was concerned. "Do you think you can do that?"

Ross waited, but she just sat on the rock, knees held to her chest, skin pale.

When she still didn't speak, he continued. "If

I can put the fact that I lost five years of my son's life behind me and forgive you…" which he wasn't sure he had, but he could either dwell on the past or embrace the future. He preferred to embrace the future "…then it really isn't too much to expect you to do the same in regard to me having accepted the position in Boston."

The fact that he couldn't say "leaving you" should tell him that she was right to blame him in some ways, because it had been about much more than just accepting the position.

His gaze met hers and he saw tears shimmering in her big eyes, saw regret and so many other things blazing in those golden-brown depths.

"Ross, I—"

"I found one!" Justice came running towards them, his hand outstretched with a rock gripped in his tiny fingers. "Look!"

"Be careful," Brielle warned, her attention completely off Ross and focused solely on their son. Her face pinched as she stood to reach for

Justice right as he lost his footing on a loose rock and tumbled forward, falling just a few feet away.

Brielle moved quicker than Ross, getting to the crying boy and lifting him into her arms. "You have to be careful on the rocks, baby. Let me check you. What hurts?"

But even before the boy sobbed out an answer Ross was already taking in the red soaking into Brielle's shirt, taking in the red that ran down Justice's leg and dripped from his hand.

The sight of blood had never bothered him. He was a doctor, for goodness' sake. But the sight of his son's blood leaving his tiny body, of blood staining Brielle's clothing, made him feel light-headed, and if he hadn't known better he'd say that was nausea welling in his stomach.

"Oh, Justice, sweetie." Cradling him in her arms, kissing the top of his head and offering tender words of comfort, Brielle examined his bleeding hand then his knee while Ross tried to pull himself together.

What was wrong with him? His knees didn't

threaten to buckle at a little blood. Or a lot of blood even. At various points during his medical career he'd dealt with nasty motor vehicle accidents, amputations, and hemorrhages that had looked like a massacre had taken place. None had twisted his stomach inside out the way the site of his son's lifeblood on the wrong side of his tiny body did.

"The cut on his hand is pretty deep, but the one on his knee is worse," Brielle said above the sound of Justice's crying. She stared at Ross as if wondering what was up with his frozen-statue routine. "What do you think? He's going to need stitches in both, isn't he?"

"I don't want 'titches." Justice's crying picked up a notch and Brielle's gaze dropped to the sobbing little boy in her lap.

"Shh, baby. It's okay," she comforted him, holding the boy even more tightly in her arms. "Mommy's got you." When Ross didn't answer her question or move, she glanced up at him and frowned. "I'll hold him while you check him,

Ross. We've got to get some pressure on to stop the bleeding. Now," she said, the last word in a raised voice, her tone warning him that he needed to get his act together.

Ross kicked into doctor mode and bent to check Justice. First his hand, which had an avulsion tear in the center of his palm where he'd tried to save himself from his fall. The jagged edge of a rock had torn into his tender flesh, lifting the skin back in a V shape. Next he checked the wide cut on his knee.

"Both are deep enough that they need sutures," he said, hating that Justice was feeling pain, would have to be anesthetized and sutured.

"That's what I thought," Brielle agreed, her eyes widening as Ross took off his T-shirt. "What are you doing?"

"Making Justice bandages. You can apply pressure while I drive him to the hospital where I can suture him. Plus, he won't be so upset if we stop the bleeding and he's not seeing blood."

Neither would Ross because the sight of blood

all over Justice and Brielle was upsetting him too. These were the two most important people in his life and one of them was hurt and there was little he could do.

He needed to be doing something, anything.

"You're going to suture him?" Brielle sounded surprised.

Surely she hadn't thought he'd let someone else do what he was more than capable of doing? Then again, after he'd been frozen for those first several seconds, perhaps she'd been justified.

"I am a medical doctor who works in the emergency room at the hospital where we will be going," he reminded them both as he ripped his T-shirt, making a rough strip of the piece he'd torn from around the hem. "I don't see a reason for someone else to suture my son, do you?"

"I don't want sutures," Justice cried pitifully between sobs, although Ross wasn't sure if the boy even knew what stitches or sutures meant. Or maybe he did. Had his son ever had sutures?

There were so many things he didn't know. So many things he wanted to learn about his son.

For the rest of their lives he'd be there, would know all the things there were to know about his child.

"I just thought…" Brielle began, then stopped, closed her eyes. "Whatever you want to do is fine. He is on my health insurance from the hospital so if you don't want to suture him, that's fine. My insurance will cover the emergency room visit."

Only after her out-of-pocket maximum and deductible were met. Or had she already met her deductible? Had Justice had other accidents? Other medical expenses earlier in the year?

Medical expenses. Expenses period. Brielle had been carrying the financial load from the beginning. Five years she'd carried the burden of being a parent alone. Lord only knew what Justice's birth and preemie care had cost. Many women would have told him, a doctor with a great income, about their pregnancy just to have him pay child support and share in the expenses. Not Brielle. Leave it to her to be one who'd bear the challenges silently, never complaining, never asking for help even if she struggled to make ends meet.

That would change.

He made a makeshift bandage and tied it round Justice's knee, putting constant pressure on the wound. "For the record, I will give you back child support. Five years' worth. More. You tell me how much and it's yours."

"Where did that come from?" Brielle's mouth fell open and she stared at him aghast. "I don't want back child support. Justice and I get along just fine by ourselves." Sensing that her tone was upsetting their son further, she softened her voice. "Now is not the time for us to be having this discussion."

She was right.

Justice was still crying in her arms, but with a lot less fervor. His decreased agitation had helped to slow the bleeding as well.

Ross took Justice's small hand in his, hating the feel of the sticky blood covering his skin. He made a bandage of sorts from the remainder of his shirt and pressed it to the wound.

"Ouch. Ouch. Ouch," Justice cried anew, jerking his hand away from Ross's, not wanting anything to touch his wound. "Mommy, make him stop."

"Here, buddy," Ross said, trying not to flinch at the pain in his son's voice, or at how he'd felt at Justice jerking away from him. "I need you to be super-brave and hold this tight against your hand. Put it right here on the wound. Squeeze it tight in your fist."

"Shh, baby, your daddy is just trying to bandage your hand." Brielle rubbed Justice's arm, trying to comfort him and trying not to look at Ross.

Would he please put his shirt back on?

Not that he could even if he wanted to. Not with it being in tatters and soaking up Justice's blood.

Her son was bleeding, albeit a lot less at this

point, and all she could think about was that Ross's chiseled chest was beautiful.

What was wrong with her?

Sure, she'd dealt with children's cuts and scrapes in the past and as an emergency room nurse she knew that Justice wasn't in any real danger. But at this moment her son was hurt and she was distracted by a gorgeous display of man-flesh. Shame on her.

And what had been up with the look they'd exchanged moments before Justice had tripped?

When it came to Ross, she really was pathetic.

She hugged her son closer to her, kissed the top of his head and wished she could take his pain on herself rather than have him suffer even the tiniest amount.

"Help him hold this on the place on his hand. I think his knee has stopped bleeding because it hasn't soaked through the material yet." He gestured to where he'd wrapped the material round Justice's knee and tied it in place using the T-shirt hem.

"I think you're right," she agreed, brushing her lips across Justice's head again. "It's gonna be okay, baby," she assured him. "I promise. We're going to take good care of you."

He'd twisted in her lap and had his head buried against her chest and his hand tucked between them. He still cried but only a little.

"Justice, son, your mother is going to carry you to the car while I pack our stuff up super-quick," Ross said, already gathering their supplies.

"Batman-quick?" Justice asked from between quivering lips.

"Faster," Ross assured him, setting everything down in a pile and reaching for Brielle's hand. "Here, let me help you to your feet."

She could stand from a sitting position while holding Justice, but doing so was becoming more and more difficult the older he got. Thinking Ross deserved bonus points for being so considerate, she took his hand while holding securely to Justice with the other. Not that her son was going anywhere anyway. Not with the tight grip he had around her neck with his arms and her waist with his legs.

Her belly flip-flopped at the skin-to-skin contact of her hand gripped tightly in Ross's firm grasp. The man exuded more electrical current than a power plant. Had to.

His fingers lingered longer than necessary, his gaze meeting hers, making her wonder what he felt when they touched. Was he bombarded with tiny zaps of excitement or drowned with memories? Or perhaps he felt nothing at all.

"I'll take Justice to the car and get him in his seat."

He still didn't let go of her hand.

"I'll meet you there," he said, his voice soft, steady, full of promises she didn't understand. Why did it sound as if he meant so much more than meeting her at the car?

She wiggled her fingers within his. His gaze dropped to their hands, as if he'd forgotten he held her. So much for her causing an electrical storm within him, the way he did her.

He let go and looked as if he was about to say something, but stopped, shook his head, and gathered up their gear.

Without another glance at him she headed towards the car with Justice. When she reached the vehicle, opened the back seat door and started to put him into his safety seat, Justice tightened his hold.

"No."

"No? Baby, I have to put you into the car so we can get your knee and hand taken care of where Mommy works."

Justice pulled his hand protectively close to his belly. "I don't want to go."

"We have to, sweetheart."

"I don't want us to leave my daddy. He might not find us again."

Brielle's heart constricted at the sincerity and concern in her son's voice, at his four-year-old logic, at what she'd deprived both Ross and her son of—each other. "Honey, we're not going to leave your daddy. He's just gathering our fishing gear so we can go fishing again some time. Together."

Despite her cajoling, Justice wouldn't let her go until Ross joined them.

"Everything okay?" he asked, eyeing them curiously as he popped the trunk with her key fob, which he'd stuck in his pocket after driving them to the lake.

"Fine," she answered, not wanting to repeat what Justice had said. At least, not until later when she and Ross could talk in private.

They needed to talk. They had a lot to say to each other. She had a lot to say to him.

Ross didn't look completely convinced, but he loaded the gear and put on a spare shirt he always carried in his hospital bag, which was stowed in her trunk, while she strapped a mostly co-operative Justice into his car seat.

Rather than get into the front seat beside Ross, she climbed into the back seat next to Justice so she could attend to him better should the bleeding worsen. Blood still hadn't soaked through the makeshift bandage on his knee, but the material held in his hand was quite messy.

Ross didn't say anything, just drove them to the hospital while she talked softly to Justice the entire ride, reassuring him about what would happen when they got to Mommy's work.

When they got to the ER, Brielle went to get Justice out of his car seat.

"I'll carry him in."

Arguing with Ross would only cause another scene in front of Justice and, really, what would be the point?

Justice was already reaching for his father to get him anyway. The sight of Justice in Ross's arms about undid her, making her legs feel weak, but she forced one foot in front of the other.

"Brielle? Dr. Lane?" Cindy's eyes were huge as they took in Brielle's bloodstained clothes and Justice wrapped around Ross. "What happened?"

"He fell. His hand and knee are cut. Not too

badly but he's going to need stitches. Can you get me set up in Bay…" he glanced around the ER to see which bay was empty "…Two?"

"Don't you think he should see the doctor on duty?" Cindy asked, eyeing them all curiously.

Ross ignored her. "After you get Bay Two set up, bring a clean scrub top for Brielle to change into."

"Right," Cindy answered, her gaze telling Brielle there was no way she was going to be put off this time.

Yeah, yeah, she got the message. All week she'd put off Cindy's questions about Ross being Justice's father, but there would be no more delay in giving an explanation.

Ross motioned for Brielle to sit on the hospital bed then he handed Justice to her.

"Son, I'm going to wash my hands, glove up, then clean your leg and hand. I need you to be very brave like I know you are, okay?"

"Like—" He named his favorite superhero.

"Exactly like him."

Determined to make his father proud, Justice

sat very still in Brielle's lap, taking in everything Ross did.

Cindy tossed a clean scrub top onto the hospital bed beside them then gloved up also. "I have everything I thought you might need set out on the tray."

"Thanks," Ross said, sliding his hands into his gloves. "If you need to go and take care of your patients, I think Brielle and I have this."

Cindy gave them a reluctant look. "You're sure?"

He nodded. "We'll be fine, but if we need you, I'll call. I know you have other patients as this was the only open bay."

She nodded, her gaze going back and forth between them. "I do, but…okay, call if you need me."

"Is he allergic to anything?" Ross asked Brielle.

"Penicillin is his only allergy."

"You're not allergic to anything," Ross remembered. "He gets that from me. I'm allergic to penicillin."

Ross sounded a bit incredulous, in awe that his

son had one of his traits. Ha, Justice had a lot more of his father than just an antibiotic allergy.

He removed the bandage from Justice's hand. The bleeding had stopped and the torn skin had lifted away from the palm.

"Ouch," Justice whimpered, then seemed to recall that he was being brave and sucked his lower lip into his mouth.

Ross rinsed the wound out with saline solution, making sure there was no foreign debris. Next he swirled iodine solution from the center of the wound outwards so as not to drag any bacteria into the wound. He picked up the anesthetic-filled syringe to numb the area prior to suturing the skin back together.

"I don't want a shot." Justice forgot about being brave and began scooting back against Brielle as tightly as his little body would go. "Mommy, don't let him give me a shot."

"I'm just going to squirt a few drops into the tear to begin with. It'll sting a little, but won't be too bad," Ross promised.

Justice still didn't want any part of the needle and Brielle had to forcibly hold his palm out while he squirmed, saying "Ouch" over and over.

Ross squirted a generous amount of anesthetic into the open wound, waited a few seconds then injected the area to the sounds of his son screaming.

Brielle cringed at her son's pain, wishing yet again she could take his pain for him.

"No. Stop! I don't like you. No. Ouch. Ouch. Daddy, stop!"

She winced at him calling Ross "Daddy" in the middle of their workplace. No way had all their co-workers not heard his cries. Then again, they all suspected something was going on between her and Ross. May as well have it all out in the open so they could move on to some new tidbit of gossip.

"You need help?" Cindy asked, poking her head into the bay, her dark gaze going straight to Brielle.

"We're fine," Brielle and Ross said at the same time.

Ross finished injecting the area and set the syringe down. Justice had already calmed down somewhat.

"Alrighty, then," the nurse said, disappearing again. "Justice, sweetie, if you need anything, you yell for me, okay?"

Justice nodded, wiping his face on Brielle's shirt. "I don't want 'titches."

"Justice, does your hand still hurt?" Ross asked.

Not looking at Ross, he nodded again.

"It does? You're sure? The magic potion medicine I put in should have put a spell on your hand and made it stop hurting completely."

Justice seemed to consider that. "Maybe it worked a little."

"That's good, son. I want you to tell me if your hand starts hurting again because the magic potion is to protect you so your hand doesn't hurt at all, okay?"

Justice eyed his hand as if expecting a glow or puff of smoke to be emitted from the wound.

Ross began to do his magic for real. He pulled

the skin flap down, lining up the wound edges as perfectly as possible then began putting in suture after suture.

On the first suture Brielle distracted Justice's attention to something elsewhere in the room rather than at what Ross was doing, and he was halfway into the second one when Justice noticed the needle.

"No." Justice tried to pull his hand away, but Brielle kept a firm grasp on it.

"You've got to hold very still, son. Remember the magic potion," Ross urged in a gentle but firm voice. He didn't stop what he was doing. "You didn't feel the first suture and you won't feel this one either. You're under the protection of magic, remember?"

Justice didn't look completely convinced but he let Ross finish, his tiny body relaxing against Brielle's. During the eighth suture his eyes closed.

"He's exhausted," she informed Ross as he tied off the last stitch and cut the Ethilon.

"No wonder. Fishing and this."

"He never even cast his line."

"Fossil hunting can be exhausting, too," he said, obviously trying to go for lightness.

Something about them being alone with their son sleeping between them made Brielle feel nervous.

Moving gently so as not to wake Justice, Brielle repositioned herself so Ross would have easy access to the cut on Justice's knee. He cut the knot, releasing the material of the makeshift bandage. The knee had bled enough to stick the fabric to the wound and he poured saline over the area to re-wet it so he could remove the fabric more easily from the area without tugging on the wound.

He repeated the steps he'd taken on Justice's palm, first cleaning the wound, then disinfecting it, then squirting anesthetic into the open wound to provide some numbness before he anesthetized the area properly by injecting anesthetic around the wound.

Justice sighed in his sleep, but Brielle comforted him, singing softly and rubbing his back as she'd done his entire life when holding him, and he didn't wake up completely.

Ross sutured the knee while Brielle watched, still singing softly to Justice.

"You're very good with him," Ross praised when he'd trimmed the Ethilon on all the sutures.

Something warm and gooey moved in her chest. "I was thinking that about you. That was brilliant with the magic potion."

"He likes magic. Almost everything we played this week ended up involving some type of spell or magic force field."

"Most children are fascinated by such things."

Ross's gaze dropped to their sleeping son nestled against her chest. "You've done a really good job with him, Brielle. A man couldn't ask for a better mother for his child."

Heat infused Brielle's face. Whether from his praise or from the way he was looking at her, she wasn't sure, just that she was getting the warm fuzzies inside and Ross was causing them.

Then again, this man had always caused her to get warm fuzzies of one kind or another.

"It was nice having you here today to help me with him," she admitted, stroking her fingers along Justice's back to occupy her hands. "Much easier than if I'd had to deal with his cuts on my own."

"I should've been there every time you needed help with him, Brielle." He grimaced, sighed, then stared directly into her eyes. "I would have been there from the beginning if I'd known."

"I know."

She did know. Only she'd wanted him to be there because he'd wanted to be there, not because he'd felt obligated to be there.

Men who stayed because they felt obligated ended up leaving and the ones left behind were all the more devastated for having believed in for ever and always.

CHAPTER TEN

ROSS CARRIED HIS son's limp body to his bedroom, waited while Brielle pulled back his bed covers, then gently laid the boy down. Brielle helped to position him in the bed, fluffing his pillow beneath him, adjusting the comforter that Ross had pulled up over the boy.

His son.

It was crazy that just two weeks before he hadn't known he had a son. Already he couldn't imagine going back to an existence without Justice. The child had won his heart completely.

He couldn't imagine going back to an existence without Brielle either.

His gaze lifted to her, caught her watching him. Her eyes were glassy, as if she fought tears. Then she lost the battle and a wet streak slid down her cheek.

"Don't cry, Brielle. He's okay." He wanted to take her into his arms, but she'd only push him away. Despite their moment of peace at the hospital, she'd clammed back up, sliding the walls she held between them back into place.

"I know." She nodded, swatting at her tears. "It's not that. It's…"

"It's…?" he prompted.

She glanced toward their sleeping son, shook her head, then quickly slipped past Ross without looking at him.

Ross watched her go, realized that more than anything he didn't want her to go, so he went after her.

"Brielle?" he said, knocking on her bedroom door.

Not having been properly latched, the door fell open. She sat on the edge of her bed, her face buried in her hands as she sobbed silently.

Ross gave in to the need to hold her.

He gave in to the need to feel her in his arms and breathe in her scent.

He gave in to everything that was inside him that said this was the woman he wanted.

Without waiting for permission, he crossed the floor, sat beside her on the bed and pulled her into his arms.

Her gaze lifted to his, startled as if she hadn't realized he was there until he held her. Had she been so lost in her misery?

"Don't cry, Brielle. I can't stand to see you cry," he said gently, brushing his fingers lighttly across her cheeks to dry her tears. "I never could."

"Don't be nice to me," she surprised him by ordering in a low but firm voice.

"Why wouldn't I be?"

"I don't deserve your kindness."

He held her tighter to him. "Sure you do."

She huffed, not meeting his eyes.

He put his hand beneath her chin, lifted it. "Look at me." When she didn't, he repeated, "Look at me, Brielle."

She looked up, meeting his gaze and wincing.

"You deserve my kindness because you are the

mother of my son, because when I chose to walk away rather than to fight for us, you didn't make the wrong choice. You gave our son life and you have done an amazing job of raising him by yourself without any help from me when I should have been by your side the whole way."

"You would have been if I'd told you. I know you would have."

"But that isn't how you wanted me, was it, Brielle?"

She shook her head. "No, I wanted…" Her voice trailed off and she averted her gaze.

"You wanted what?" he prompted, tilting her chin, realizing that the distance between their mouths was closing. He could feel her breath teasing his lips, could feel the warmness of her mouth beckoning him.

"You," she answered simply, closing her eyes and looking as if she was in agony.

Agony that Ross understood. He was feeling pretty agonized himself.

"I wanted you," she whispered, eyes still shut.

He leaned forward the slightest amount, putting his lips in direct contact with hers, and ended his agony.

Her lips felt amazing against his.

Her eyes shot open, searched his for answers that he doubted she'd find because he didn't have answers, not to any of the questions shining in her eyes.

All he knew was that he had never stopped wanting this woman. That for five years he'd wanted her but had been too stubborn to admit that he'd needed her all those years before.

He needed her now.

Her mouth remained perfectly still and he couldn't stand it. He wanted to taste her, to put his tongue into the sweet recesses of her mouth and conquer all.

As if sensing his need, she parted her lips and Ross growled his pleasure.

"You taste so good," he groaned, supping on her lower lip. "So perfect."

"Don't talk," she ordered low against his mouth. "Please, just don't say anything. Just...just kiss me."

Ross might have stopped to analyze her comment had he been thinking straight. But he hadn't been thinking straight from the moment he'd taken her into his arms.

No, longer than that. He hadn't been thinking straight for years, since the first time he'd laid eyes on his roommate's kid sister who had just been finishing nursing school and had literally taken his breath away. What had happened to make him forget that?

To forget how she'd affected him? How he'd instantly known he'd have her? Yet he'd been the one to walk away, and for what?

At the moment nothing seemed as pressing as loving this woman, familiarizing himself again with everything about her.

Her lips. Her mouth. Her face. Her neck.

Oh, her neck. How he'd always loved her neck.

What a sweet arch she had.

When he kissed her collar bone, slid his hands under the borrowed hospital scrub top to push the material out of his way, he groaned. Brielle had more curves and slopes than a geometry text-book.

Her fingers tangled in his hair as he breathed in the lovely scent between her breasts.

Fuller, he thought. Her breasts were fuller than when they'd been together before. Had time or childbirth done that?

Either way, he was going to reap their bounty.

His fingers found the clasp to her bra and freed her beautiful breasts. He stared in appreciation. "You're beautiful, Brielle. So beautiful."

"No talking," she reminded him, pulling his mouth back to hers and kissing him so thoroughly, so hungrily that the constriction of his shorts grew painful and he had to adjust himself.

He pushed her back on her bed, leaned forward and kissed her belly, then lifted his T-shirt over his head, wanting to feel his skin against hers, his body against hers with nothing between them.

"You're the one who is beautiful," she murmured, tracing her fingers down his chest. "You always were so beautiful, Ross."

He started to correct her, to tell her he was a man and far far from beautiful. Then her fingers found their way to his waist. All he could do was suck in his breath in eager anticipation of what she'd do next.

No, he thought. This wasn't about him. It was about Brielle. About how much he wanted to make her feel good, about how much he wanted to give her pleasure. He wanted Brielle so caught up in him that she was as hungry for him as he was for her.

Hungrier. Starved.

His hand covered hers just as she slid his zipper down and he shook his head.

Her brow lifted in question.

By way of answer he tugged on her elastic-waisted shorts, sliding them over the curve of her hips, down her toned thighs and calves, and tossed them onto her floor.

Lying on the bed in only her bright pink cotton panties, Brielle was easily the most beautiful sight his eyes had ever been lucky enough to behold.

Beautiful.

His.

He may have been stupid enough not to acknowledge the connection between them when he'd been younger, but now he knew. He and Brielle were meant to be together. Always and for ever.

This time he was wise enough to embrace that fact rather than try to run from something so powerful.

Love.

He loved Brielle.

Always had. Always would.

He slipped his fingers beneath her panties and slid them down the same path as her shorts.

Immediately, he realized he'd been wrong.

Looking at her, completely naked, lying on the bed waiting for his touch, that was the most beautiful sight he'd ever been lucky enough to behold.

She watched him, her skin flushed with desire, her eyes half-lidded and her lips parted.

So beautiful.

He ran his hands over her legs, going slowly, enjoying every glide of his skin across hers, growing more and more excited with the goose-bumps that prickled her skin at his touch, at the way her nipples puckered and strained upwards, eager to touch him, to be touched by him.

As much as he wanted to explore every inch of her body, slowly and surely, kissing her breasts, bringing her to the brink of pleasure and then toppling her over time and again, he couldn't do it.

Because he couldn't resist the tantalizing pull of between her legs.

He bent, dipped his tongue between her pretty pink lips, and suckled the swollen flesh.

"Ross," she murmured, her fingers back in his hair, working across his scalp as her hips writhed against the thrust of his tongue.

He laved her most sensitive part until her breath

came in short pants and she said his name over and over as if chanting a magic spell all her own.

Perhaps she had because certainly he felt enchanted, under her spell, as if some magical force was at work making him completely and totally hers.

She arched off the bed, curled her fingers tightly into his hair then cried out softly with her orgasm.

Hearing her pleasure, seeing her reaction to his touch, feeling her, tasting her overwhelmed Ross's senses and he lost control.

Lost control of his mind and his body.

He finished the job she'd started, shucking his shorts off in record time and moving over her, positioning his body, then without hesitation slid home to where he'd always belonged.

With Brielle.

Brielle closed her eyes at the sheer pleasure moving through her body.

Every touch of Ross's hand against her lit fires

that had burned low for too many years. Every brush of his mouth against her body started infernos only he could quench.

Now, feeling him stretching her, filling her up with him, she wanted to cry from the joy of it. Then again, crying was what had started this.

No, she wouldn't think about the emotions that had assuaged her when she'd gone to her room and given in to the tears. For the moment she was just going to be greedy, to take what his body was giving, to feel all the things she'd had denied her for five years.

Five long, lonely years since she'd made love to this man. To any man. Five long, forlorn years when she'd loved him, missed him, wanted him to miraculously reappear in her life, sweep her off her feet and tell her he felt exactly the same way about her.

Never had she actually believed he would.

Not really.

Or had she?

Sure, there had been a part of her that had

dreamed, hoped, but she'd kept that part buried so she could survive day by day with a big chunk of her heart missing.

She'd focused on Justice, Vann, her job. She'd been happy, even if she'd always known something was missing. Someone. Ross.

But here he was. Buried deep inside her, his gorgeous body moving against hers, thrusting deeper and deeper until rational thought was becoming more and more difficult, until all she wanted was to lose herself in him.

His lips marauded hers, as if her mouth provided him with the necessities of life itself and he was a dying man in need of sustenance.

His hands caressed her, then supported his body above hers where he angled himself, driving even deeper into her, but where he could watch her beneath him.

From her vantage point she admired the chiseled lushness of his chest, of his cut abdomen. She wanted to reach out and touch him as she had earlier, but her insides began to melt and she could only curl her fingers into tight fists. First she melted only at the very core of her, but then she liquefied in a spiraling outward motion that built in momentum until every nerve cell was rocked with the force of a tornado turning her insides out in a pleasurable explosion.

She gripped her bed covers. Her fingers clenched and unclenched. Wave after wave of glorious spasms shook her body. She arched into Ross, then bit her tongue to keep from crying out with the enormity of the orgasm that hit her.

Total. Orgasmic. Meltdown.

But he wasn't through. Oh, no. Just as she crashed over the pinnacle of her pleasurable ride, he jetted her right back up by taking her nipple in his mouth and giving her a hard suckle, all the while imprinting her body over and over with him.

She lost count of how many times he brought her up, let her fall just a little so she could appreciate the next ascent to an even higher crest. Over and over until she was positive her brain would never function again. That all of her body had completely short-circuited from the lightning running through her and she would remain a sizzled, spent gob of ooey-gooey goop.

When she felt the change in his pace, the tightening of his abdominal muscles, the tension pouring from every pore of his body, she arched into his thrust, meeting his rhythm, welcoming the rush of pleasure filling her body as, that time, it was her name crossing his lips in a possessive growl.

His body glistening with sweat, he virtually collapsed onto her, kissing her cheek. "Perfect."

Not perfect, but his words and the way he hugged her to him, rolled them over to where she was lying on him rather than vice versa, holding her close and managing to keep their bodies joined throughout the maneuver as if he couldn't bear to part from her yet, warmed a part of her that had been cold for a long time. A part she'd buried in the icy recesses of the past to keep the pain from destroying her.

Their bodies stuck together and she hid her face in the groove of his neck, breathing hard. Her heart pounded so forcefully that every finger and toe throbbed in pulsating cadence. Her entire body throbbed, ebbed, flowed.

The intensity began to recede and her brain began to reboot itself, to register the impact of what they'd just done. Her sweaty, spent body was stretched out over Ross's long, hard body, both of them out of breath, both of them clinging to the other.

Crack after crack she heard the thaw, felt the reality of her vulnerability to Ross become more and more exposed.

Barely here two weeks and she'd already spread her legs and welcomed him inside her body. Did that make her easy?

Perhaps, but if so, she was only easy for this one man because he was the only one with the power to move her so. The only man she'd ever wanted.

Was she wrong to have taken what he'd offered? To have given in to the need within her to be with him?

She hadn't planned on this. Had planned just the opposite, especially with him living with her and Justice. They didn't need to be doing this or touching at all. There were too many obstacles between them as it was. Sex would just end up being one more.

Sex?

Was that what they'd just done? Had sex?

Never in the past when she'd been with Ross had she questioned that they were making love. Never.

But then he'd left her and that had changed everything, had changed her. He may have been irresistible, he may have exposed her vulnerable heart, but no longer was she the naive girl who'd fallen in love with him and given him her heart and body.

This time she knew that Ross wasn't playing for keeps and the good thing was that even if he was, she wasn't.

He'd permanently cured her of that.

She refused to be like her mother and that one thing would keep her safe from Ross, even if nothing else would.

Despite his tight hold, she rolled off him, lay flat on her back and stared at the ceiling, each breath still coming hard and fast. Ross's breathing was coming even harder, faster from his position next to her.

He took her hand, squeezed, dropped their clasped fingers to the bed, and took several deep breaths, before blowing everything she'd just thought right out of the water.

"We should get married."

Ross didn't have to turn his head to know Brielle was staring at him as if he'd lost his mind. He felt her horrified glare. Felt the shock pouring from her every pore as she gawked at him.

Not exactly the reaction a man hoped for when discussing marriage with a woman.

"We have sex once and you say we should get

married?" She sounded incredulous, as if he'd spoken in a foreign tongue about something impossible and far-fetched.

"Not just once," he reminded her, expecting her to point out that it had only been once in the past five years.

A deep V cut into her forehead and she just continued to stare at him as if he'd lost his mind. "All those times that we did so much more years ago, when I loved you with all my heart, and none of the previous times inspired you to want to walk down the aisle with me. Am I so good now that after a single time you feel the need to shroud me in white and listen to wedding bells peal? Pardon me if I don't buy it."

He rolled onto his side so he could see her more easily. "Sarcasm? Really? After what we just shared you give me sarcasm when I ask you a serious question?"

She didn't so much as flinch. "You asked nothing."

Ross frowned. Hadn't he?

"You want me to get down on my knee and propose, Brielle? Would that put a nice smile on your face? Would that make you happy? Because if that's what you want, I will."

"No." Her gaze narrowed and he regretted his snappy comment. Only hadn't she just been right there with him, experiencing the same things he'd experienced? Sex between them had always been good, but that had been… He searched for a word and still failed to define what he'd just shared with Brielle.

"I don't want to marry you." Her words sliced into his thoughts.

"What?" He sat up, stared down into her stubborn face, not quite believing she was serious. She'd loved him, was the mother of his child, had practically beat him over the head with bridal magazines just a few years before, and now she didn't want to marry him?

"You heard me."

He glared at her, trying to read her expression, trying to decipher what was really going on behind her words. "Is this your idea of retribution because I didn't jump on board five years ago when you were trying to shotgun me down the aisle?"

She sat up too, glared much more fiercely than anything he could pull off. "No, this is me not wanting to marry you and saying so."

"You used to want to marry me," he reminded her, not liking how his euphoria of just moments before had completely dissipated and was being replaced with something dark and ugly.

She shrugged. "What I used to want is irrelevant to what I want today. I don't want to be your wife."

He eyed her, noting the slight quiver to her lower lip, the rapid pulse at her throat. "People don't change that much."

"Exactly," she agreed, although he didn't understand what she was agreeing to. She crossed her arms over her breasts then, seeming to realize she was naked, she yanked her bed covers over her body. "You are the one man I won't ever marry. Got it?"

What the…?

"Why not?" He didn't bother keeping his voice low because…well, just because, although he remembered too late that his son was just down the hall and the last thing he wanted was Justice to hear them arguing. "Why not?" he repeated much more softly, hoping she'd take his cue and keep her voice down too.

"Justice."

"Now I really don't understand. Our son is why you won't marry me? Perhaps you didn't notice but the boy likes me and needs his father, me, in his life."

"I never said he doesn't need you or that you shouldn't be in his life. And of course he likes you. You've showered him with attention and gifts. Why wouldn't he like you?"

"You make the fact that I bought my son a few things this week sound as if I was trying to bribe him. Thanks to you, I have five years to make up for so forgive me if I go a little crazy here at the beginning and want to see my kid's face light up a few times. I've only been a father, that I knew of, for a little over a week. Forgive me if I don't get everything just perfect. I'm learning as I go. I think I'm owed a little slack there, don't you?"

Gaze downward cast and pulling her comforter over her body, she nodded. "I'm sure you are. I can't change the past any more than you can. What's done is done. If I'd known you'd have wanted to be a part of Justice's life, I'd—"

"Oh, spare me your sob story," he interrupted, frustrated, angry, pulling on his underwear and shorts. "We both know the truth. You didn't tell me to punish me for leaving."

"I didn't," she gasped, sounding horrified.

"You did. Did it give you satisfaction to know that you'd given birth to my child, were raising my son all without me being any the wiser? Did you feel as if retribution had been served every time you looked at him and knew my eyes had never even seen him?"

Her mouth fell open, her gaze narrowed, and

her eyes flickered with anger. "Get out!" she ordered, pointing toward her bedroom door.

"The truth hurts, doesn't it?"

"Get out!" she repeated, grabbing her clothes and dressing in haste then tossing his T-shirt at him. "Get out of my bedroom, out of my house, and out of my life! You aren't wanted here. Do you hear me? We did just fine without you and don't need you here. I don't want you here!"

"As if you could make me stay," he countered, sliding on his T-shirt, wondering how the magic of moments before had morphed into something so ugly, wondering why he wasn't stopping this because deep down he knew he didn't want to go.

"You'll be hearing from my lawyers," he said, instead of begging her to forgive him for his pride. "I tried to do this the nice way, even asked you to marry me, but you had to be difficult, didn't you?" Or was he the one being difficult? Had he rushed things? No, he wanted to marry the mother of his five-year-old child. If anything, he was behind the times. But she no longer wanted to marry him. A fresh pain stabbed his heart. "Have it your way. We won't get married, but my son will live with me. Not just every other weekend."

"No," she cried, her face paling to a pasty white as she dropped onto the edge of the bed as if her legs were no longer strong enough to support her. She sat, staring at him in horror. "You can't do that."

He wouldn't do that. She was a good mother. Justice needed her.

"Oh, yes, Brielle." He barely recognized his own voice, but defensive pain pushed him down a different path than the one he wanted to travel. No, he didn't need to feel sorry for her. He needed to remember what she'd done to him, to their son, and why? Because she'd had some misguided notion that he should have married her without knowing and since he hadn't agreed, she wouldn't marry him at all? She didn't deserve his consideration. She sure hadn't shown him any. "You had five years. I want what you stole from me. Five years."

Red splotched her pale cheeks. "No judge is going to give you that!"

"No?" He arched his brow, too hurt and angry to stop his bitter words. "You think you can provide that boy with a better life than I can? Think again."

"I have provided him with a good home, a good life. I give him everything he needs," she insisted.

"No." He shook his head with disdain. "You didn't. You didn't give him the father he obviously craves and needs. Me."

With that he gave her one last look of disgust then left her bedroom. He wanted to slam her door. Lord, how he wanted the satisfaction of slamming her bedroom door. Instead, in deference to their hopefully still sleeping son, he closed the door behind him with a resounding click that echoed through his mind as he walked down the hallway.

Away from Brielle.

Why did that feel so wrong?

CHAPTER ELEVEN

BRIELLE HAD DREADED going in to the hospital because she'd have to see Ross. There would be no way to avoid seeing him in the emergency department with them both working there.

Perhaps she shouldn't have bothered worrying.

He seemed as intent on ignoring her as she was on ignoring him.

She'd not seen him since he'd stormed out of her apartment three days before. A mere week at her house and everywhere she looked she saw him, had flashbacks of seeing him there with Justice, of hearing his laughter, of his scent filling her home, of just knowing he was there.

As much as she missed him, Justice missed him more.

The day after their argument Ross had called and very tersely asked to speak to Justice. She'd handed her son the phone, wanted to listen in, but had forced herself to go to the kitchen for a moment to give her son a minute of privacy. When she'd come back into the room, Justice had set the phone down and gone to his room. She'd picked the phone up but the line had been dead.

The silence at the end of the phone a harsh reminder of the void in her life.

Justice hadn't mentioned what Ross had said, but he'd been full of questions.

"Where's my daddy?

"Why did my daddy have to go far away?

"Is my daddy coming home soon?

"We need to go find my daddy."

Justice couldn't seem to focus on anything except the void Ross's disappearance from their house had left. Even Vann had commented on it when he'd come to visit them. Her brother hadn't said too much about Ross. He'd just listened to her give a glossed-over version of what had happened because she sure wasn't telling him she'd been stupid enough to have sex with Ross. Then

Vann had told her to be patient and forgiving, that Ross was dealing with a lot and probably just needed some time.

That hadn't sat well and so they'd opted to not discuss Ross for the rest of her brother's visit.

Only Justice had grilled his uncle on Ross's whereabouts.

Her poor son. She'd wanted to protect him. Instead, she'd been stupid, given in to her own passion for Ross and ended up ruining every thing.

Had they been destined to fail from the beginning? The past too painful for them to forge any kind of amicable relationship in the present?

For Justice's sake, she hoped not.

Part of her had been on edge, expecting to receive a court summons regarding custody. Probably she would as, realistically, those things took much longer than a few days to set into motion.

She wouldn't fight him regarding sharing their son. Justice needed both of his parents. But she would fight till her dying breath if he attempted to take Justice from her completely.

Maybe he did have the right since he'd missed five years of his son's life, but he'd destroy her if he denied her access to Justice.

Somehow she knew he wouldn't, that he'd only do what he thought was right for Justice. He himself had said that she was a good mother, that she'd done a good job with Justice. Despite their argument, she knew Ross wouldn't remove Justice completely from her life. Not for her sake but for Justice's.

"Bay Three needs vitals, to be hooked up to telemetry and cardiac enzymes drawn." Ross's order cut into her mind's meanderings. "His information says he has chest pain, so why isn't someone with him?"

Good point. She'd seen the nurse call him back immediately after he'd signed in to the emergency department, stating he had chest pain, but that had been a few minutes ago and the nurse had disappeared.

"Yes, sir." Brielle put down the clipboard she was making notes on, turning it upside down to prevent passersby from being able to see her patient's recorded information. She didn't bother to explain that Bay Three was another nurse's patient. If something was going on in the emergency room, whoever was available took care of it regardless of who'd been assigned to the patient.

She wasn't sure where the nurse had gone during the middle of triaging the patient, but Brielle would finish it and carry out Ross's orders.

When she stepped into the bay, she introduced herself to the fifty-three-year-old man, who was holding his chest.

Ross was right. The man shouldn't have been left alone. His face was ruddy, his skin clammy, and he had a nervous, wild-eyed appearance that set warning bells off in Brielle's head.

"Mr. Cook, do you have anyone with you?"

The man shook his head. "No, I drove myself here."

Scary thought for him to have been behind the wheel of a car, but she smiled, wanting to keep him calm and definitely not wanting to raise his anxiety level.

She assisted in removing his shirt, put an automatic blood-pressure cuff on his left upper arm, and began hooking the telemetry to him. He had a hairy body and the leads wouldn't stick. She quickly shaved the hair in the appropriate spots and stuck the leads on, getting good adherence.

She pressed the button, turning on the heart monitor. What she saw widened her eyes.

His erratic pulse was registering anywhere from one hundred and forty to two hundred beats per minute in a horribly irregular rhythm.

"Dr. Lane?" she called, keeping her voice calm. "I have Mr. Cook's heart monitor started if you'd like to check him."

Knowing she wouldn't have called him if he didn't need to come immediately, Ross stepped into the bay, saw what had concerned her and began taking action.

"Give him…" He named the appropriate medication and dosage. He rattled off more orders and Brielle made a mental note of each one, even as she began drawing up the medication to administer it.

As the man didn't have an intravenous line in yet, Ross sat down next to him and started the IV himself.

Again, Brielle had to question where the nurse assigned to the patient had disappeared to. Ross got the line started and she pushed the medication in.

"I want Cardiology here now," Ross told her, then turned to Mr. Cook. "At the minimum, you're going to need to be admitted so we can check you out really well to see what is going on. Right now your heart is out of rhythm. The medications the nurse gave you will help keep you from developing a blood clot and will help the heart not have to work quite so hard until the heart specialist gets here to evaluate you."

The man nodded as if he understood but rather than answer Ross, he closed his eyes.

The monitor's beeping became a constant steady drone.

A drone that caused adrenaline to surge in any medical professional's body.

Brielle's stomach fell and her own adrenaline skyrocketed.

Mr. Cook had flat-lined.

Beginning CPR, Ross called the code as Brielle grabbed the crash cart. She prepared the defibrillator and handed the paddles to Ross.

"All clear," he said, and immediately gave the man an electric shock with the paddles.

Nothing.

Hearing the code call, Cindy joined them and began giving the man breaths of air via a hand-held air bag as they performed two-man CPR. Brielle took over compressions while they waited for the defibrillator to recharge.

"Again," Ross said, the second the machine was ready to deliver another charge. "All clear."

Cindy and Brielle stepped back. Ross put the

paddles to the man's chest. The man's body jerked from the jolt of electricity.

Brielle held her breath, waiting, hoping.

His heart gave a resounding beep on the monitor. Then another. And another.

"Thank God," she breathed, knowing that the man was far from out of danger as at any moment the tide could turn.

"Give him…" Ross named the medication and Brielle nodded, turning to grab the injectible medication from the crash cart. He turned to Cindy. "Get Cardiology here stat."

"Yes, sir. Dr. Heather Abellano is in the CCU. I saw her earlier." Cindy glanced toward Brielle then headed out of the partitioned exam room.

Brielle continued to monitor the patient, all too aware that Ross was watching her. Okay, so really he was observing the patient, but she could sense his gaze shift to her every few seconds.

But he didn't say a single word to her. Not one.

Within minutes, Dr. Abellano was in the room, examining Mr. Cook and having him transferred to the cardiac care unit for further evaluation and treatment.

Once Mr. Cook was on his way, Brielle sighed in relief, glad her shift was almost over and she could go home to Justice.

She glanced toward Ross. He was scribbling on Mr. Cook's emergency room encounter, no doubt documenting the man's code, stabilization, and transfer.

He glanced up, caught her staring at him. His brow lifted, but she only looked away. What did he expect? For her to say something? What was she supposed to say that they hadn't already said?

Ross signed his name at the bottom of the emergency room encounter, trying to focus on the task at hand and not on the woman across the room restocking the crash cart.

The woman who'd turned his life upside down.

He couldn't say that he regretted his decision to come to Bean's Creek. If he hadn't, he'd never have known about Justice. He'd done the right thing.

About coming here, if nothing else.

On everything else he just wasn't sure.

Everything had seemed so clear in his mind when he'd stormed out of her house.

He'd had to leave.

Yet hadn't he done exactly what she'd expected all along? Left when things got sticky?

He wasn't a quitter, or the type of man who walked away from a problem. He'd have labeled himself a problem-solver, not a runner.

Yet perhaps Brielle was justified to think that way of him, because with her he hadn't stuck around when things got muddled.

But unlike in the past, he hadn't left with no intention of returning. Over the past few days he'd made major life decisions. Decisions that he'd needed to make with a clear head.

Apparently, a clear head and being near Brielle didn't go hand in hand. Not for him. She made him crazy.

She made him alive.

More alive than at any other point in his life.

Every emotion was more intense, more real, more vivid with Brielle back in his life, and that's where he wanted her, in his life.

He probably should have stayed, camped out on her sofa until they'd both cooled off. Instead, he'd flown to Boston, arranged to sell his practice to his partners, put his apartment on the market and tied up loose ends because he wouldn't be moving back at the end of his three months in Bean's Creek.

Regardless of what happened between him and Brielle, he was staying in North Carolina, was staying where his family was, Justice and Brielle.

What was happening between them?

What did he want to happen?

Hadn't that thought been foremost in his mind over the past few days? What was it he wanted more than anything?

Not what currently was, that was for sure.

His skin crawled every time he caught her looking at him with her big sad eyes. He wanted her eyes smiling, her lips laughing, her world a better place because he was in her life. What he didn't want was to cause her stress and grief.

But he was going to be a part of Justice's daily life.

He'd missed five years of his son's life. He wouldn't miss any more. He missed that kid.

He missed Brielle.

He glanced at where she was talking to the nurse who'd just returned from helping transport Mr. Cook. Brielle looked tired, stressed, as if she hadn't been sleeping well, and he knew he was to blame.

He wanted to wrap his arms around her and tell her he wanted to come home.

Home? Was that how he thought of her quaint little house? Home was where the heart was.

His heart was wherever Brielle and Justice were.

Yes, he wanted to go home.

Which meant he and Brielle needed to talk. No coercion or threats on his part regarding custody of Justice, though. He wanted her to invite him to come back. For her to tell him she'd missed him as much as he'd missed her.

He wanted her to love him as much as he loved her.

As much as she had loved him once upon a time.

If she'd loved him once, he'd win her love again. He knew Brielle. She wasn't the kind to love lightly. She'd given him her heart and he was going to stake his future happiness on the fact that she'd never gotten it back completely, otherwise she wouldn't have made love with him.

They had made love. Yes, the chemistry between them was phenomenal, but their connection went way beyond physical.

Love really was the most powerful thing in the world.

Why question himself?

He knew what he wanted.

The time apart had cleared that up for him and he had no doubts about the direction he wanted his future to take.

He glanced at his watch. Their shift was almost over. Thank God. Today had been a killer day. Or maybe it had been the tension between him and Brielle that had made him feel that way.

He'd known that at the end of their shift he'd talk to her, get down on his knees and beg her to open her heart to him.

Somehow he would convince her that he deserved a second chance, deserved her love, deserved the opportunity to love and cherish her and their son for the rest of their lives.

He put his hand in his scrub pocket. His fingers traced over a velvet box. Why had he brought the trinket with him? It wasn't as if he'd do anything with it at the hospital, yet he hadn't wanted to leave it at the apartment he'd returned to late last night either.

Brielle came over to the station where he sat and picked up a clipboard.

"I'd like to see Justice tonight."

"Fine."

Ross cringed. He really didn't like that word.

"Could I take you both to dinner?"

She hesitated only a second. "No, but you are welcome to spend time with Justice, either taking him to dinner or playing with him at my house."

"But I'm not welcome to spend time with you?"

She shook her head. "The less time we spend together, the better for Justice's sake."

"Why's that?"

"Because us being together is like mixing fire and gasoline. We can't coexist."

"We coexisted for years. Quite well," he reminded her.

"That was before."

"Before?"

"Justice."

"Justice is all the more reason for us to coexist."

Which was exactly why Brielle couldn't even try. She couldn't be her mother. Hadn't she seen the devastation that forcing a man into marriage caused?

"You are welcome to see him. He misses you."

"I miss him." Ross raked his fingers through his dark hair. "Look, Brielle…" he glanced around the for once almost empty emergency department "…we need to talk. Not here. Not at your place with Justice there. Just you and me."

"I don't see the point."

"Then give me the opportunity to show you the point."

She sighed. As much as she didn't want to have the conversation with him, she knew that eventually she'd have to. He was her son's father and would always be a part of her life.

"Fine. We'll talk, but I have to pick Justice up from his preschool after-care when I get off work, so not tonight."

He seemed ready to argue with her, but the vibration of her cellular phone in her pocket and her pulling the phone out to check the number stopped him.

She rarely got a phone call at work.

The preschool.

"Hello."

"Hey, Brielle, this is Rachel. I don't know how to tell you this, but…Justice is missing."

Brielle's heart stopped. "Missing? What do you mean, missing?"

"We've looked every where at the school and can't find him. He's gone."

Brielle couldn't say another word, could barely stand. Her gaze met Ross's concerned one and she held the phone out to him in a hand that visibly shook.

He took the phone. "This is Dr. Ross Lane. What's going on?"

Brielle moved in a daze as Ross had her get her purse while he informed Administration that they were both leaving. Fortunately, it was close enough to shift change that their replacements were already at the hospital.

Wordlessly, she climbed into the passenger seat of his car, rode to the preschool with panic and fear foremost in her heart and mind.

Missing. Justice was missing.

Ross had called the police the moment he'd

hung up from the preschool, reported what the preschool teacher had told him. Although not enough time had passed for them to file an official missing-person report, they were sending an officer to meet them at the preschool.

When Ross reached across the car seat and took her hand into his, she didn't pull away. Somewhere in the horror of the moment she registered that his hand trembled. Yet she drew great strength from knowing he was there, that he was with her and she didn't have to face this alone.

She acknowledged she was in shock.

She moved through the next thirty minutes without anything really registering except that she ached inside as she'd never ached before.

Ross stayed at her side, holding her, letting her cry, helping her when her hands shook too much for her to remove the photo of Justice from her wallet to give to the police.

"We'll have all units on the look out and give you folks a call if we hear anything. I suggest you go home and see if he's gone there."

Hope lit in Brielle's heart. Was it possible that Justice had gone home?

Had he run away from the preschool? Her mind had gone in a hundred directions, all of which involved someone snatching her son.

But what if Justice had left on his own?

Why would he do that?

She glanced at Ross, the truth dawning and hope growing that Justice was okay. "He's not at home."

"How do you know that?"

"He's gone to find you."

Ross's brows lifted. "But I told him I'd come back, that I was only going to be in Boston for a few days."

He'd gone to Boston? Why?

"Obviously he didn't want to wait a moment longer to find you. He kept saying we needed to go find you."

She closed her eyes, remorse filling her.

Oh, Justice. She should have taken more notice of his questions, known that her brilliant son would be a person of action, not waiting around for something he wanted desperately.

"We'll check at local bus stops and contact the local taxi services to see if anyone remembers seeing him," the officer informed them, putting a call in to the communication center.

Brielle nodded then jumped as her phone started ringing. Oh, please, oh, please, oh, please, be Justice, she prayed.

Vann's number showed on the screen. She winced. She hadn't even thought to call her brother. Vann. Justice would have gone to Vann for help.

She hit the answer icon on her phone. "Is Justice with you?"

"Yeah, he just showed up. Alone. What's up?"

Her body sagged with relief. "Thank God. Oh, Vann, thank God."

"He's with Vann?" Ross asked, relief evident in his voice as well.

She nodded, listening to her brother explain how Justice had shown up at the hospital where he worked in a taxi, stating he needed Vann's help to find his daddy.

Brielle started crying and couldn't quit. Not silent tears but full-out, shaking-her-entire-body sobs.

Ross wrapped his arms around her. "Shh, baby, it's going to be okay. He's all right. He's with Vann and he's bringing him back to us."

After letting the police and the preschool know what had happened, they left and went to Brielle's house to wait for Vann to arrive.

"I won't stop him from seeing you. Ever," Brielle informed him when they were sitting on her kitchen bar stools. Ross had forced her to sit, and drink a glass of water. She knew he was just trying to distract her while they waited, anything to help pass the time.

"I know. I feel the same. He needs us both."

Swiping at her eyes, which were wet again, she nodded. "He does." She glanced at Ross, met his red-rimmed eyes and realized that her eyes weren't the only ones that were wet. "Oh, Ross. I'm so sorry. For everything."

She stood, wrapped her arms around him, felt the comfort of his arms around her. How long they stood there she wasn't sure. Just that they clung to each other, comforting and being comforted.

"Forgive me, Ross. Forgive me for not telling you I was pregnant," she sobbed, needing to tell him everything. "I wanted you to want me for me, not because I was pregnant."

"I did want you."

"I mean for ever, Ross." She pulled back, stared at him and buried her pride. "Call me silly or old-fashioned or a hopeless romantic, but I wanted you to sweep me off my feet because you loved me and wanted to spend the rest of your life with me. What I didn't want was for you to feel obligated to marry me because I was pregnant and the kid sister of your best friend."

"I was an idiot, Brielle. I should have known that something was going on when you started acting so different." He put his hands on her shoulders, gripped her tight. "I didn't understand and rather than fight for you, for us, I panicked and ran."

"You didn't run. Boston was a great opportunity. You'd have been a fool to turn it down."

"Leaving you made me a bigger fool."

"No, you didn't want the same things I did so you staying would have been worse."

"Tell me, Brielle, when did you start wanting to get married? Before or after you found out you were pregnant?"

She thought back. "From the moment I first kissed you I knew I wanted to marry you."

"But there wasn't a rush until you found out you were pregnant, right?"

"I always figured we'd wait until you were finished with your residency program and were in practice. Honestly, I was so happy being with you I never put a time frame on when we'd take that next step."

"Until nature forced you to put a time frame on it."

"I was wrong to not tell you outright. I just…" Her voice trailed off.

"You just wanted me to do the right thing and give you your happily-ever-after. Only I didn't have all the facts, Brielle. Not like you did, and I didn't understand the sudden rush and the personality changes and you shutting me out when we'd always been so close and of the same mind."

"I should have told you."

He nodded. "Yes, you should have." He took a deep breath. "But having spent several hours earlier this week talking to your brother, I can understand why you didn't, why you wanted more from me."

"You talked to Vann?"

"Yesterday, when my flight landed, I went straight to him. We had dinner, talked."

"I always regretted that your friendship with him ended because of me."

"I regretted that our friendship ended, but that

wasn't your fault, Brielle. It was mine, because I let it end without fighting to save it, just as I let my relationship with you end without fighting for it. I can only blame ignorance and youth and stupidity."

"You're not ignorant or stupid, Ross."

"Letting our relationship go wasn't wise, Brielle. Not when it meant losing the only woman I've ever loved."

She swallowed, waited for him to say more, desperate to hear his next words.

"I did date, Brielle. I went through a lot of women, fast, out of sheer desperation. None of them could hold my attention. None of them were you."

The thought of him with other women pained her, but she only bit her lip, keeping silent, knowing he had more to say.

"I met a woman, a doctor I worked with. Theoretically, she was ideal, the perfect mate, and I considered asking her to marry me."

Brielle's heart squeezed. There had been someone special in his life? Thinking of him with other women who were meaningless was one thing. Thinking of him with a woman he'd loved quite another.

"But I couldn't bring myself to do it. You were on my mind more often than not and I kept wondering what you were doing, if you'd ever married, if there was any chance the sparks would still fly between us. I'd wake up from dreaming of you, reach over to hold you, and you wouldn't be there. I'd convince myself that we'd had our chance and only a fool looked back."

He gave a low laugh. "Then I went to this conference in Philadelphia, saw Vann, and instantly knew that I couldn't move on to whatever my future was supposed to be until I saw you again."

He'd thought of her? Dreamed of her? Possibly in the same moments she'd been thinking and dreaming of him?

"Quite casually Vann mentioned that the hospital where you worked was going to have a temporary opening in the emergency room when one of the doctors went on maternity leave. I jumped on it, knowing that just seeing you wasn't going to be enough. The anticipation of seeing you again was eating me alive. You want to talk about silly, hopeless romantic?" He gave an ironic smirk. "When I saw you all I wanted was for you to drop everything and run across the ER, meet me half-way, and throw yourself into my arms."

She swallowed the lump forming in her throat, couldn't quite believe her ears. "You wanted that?"

"I wanted you. I've always wanted you. And before you launch into a tirade about sex, I don't just mean physically, Brielle. I mean you. When I lost you five years ago, I lost a part of myself, and I want that part back."

Her heartbeat thudded in her ears, making hearing difficult, making thinking difficult. "What are you saying?"

"That my heart is yours."

"And you want it back?"

"Asking for it back isn't really what I'm trying to say." He paused, sighed. "When I said we should get married the other night, I wasn't thinking of Justice, or even you."

"What were you thinking of?"

"Me," he answered simply. "I was thinking of me."

"You?"

"I wanted you always, Brielle. I wanted you to be mine for all time. Not because of our son but because I don't want to be without you ever again. I need you." He put his hands on her cheeks, stared straight into her eyes. "I love you, Brielle Winton. I always have. I always will."

Ross waited for Brielle to speak, for her to say anything in response to the outpouring of his heart. Her lips parted then she seemed to lose strength and leaned on him, resting against his chest.

"Oh, Ross."

He held her, kissing the top of her head, wondering what "Oh, Ross" meant.

"You don't have to marry me, you know. I'm yours anyway. I always have been."

"I know I don't have to marry you, Brielle. But you're not listening to what I'm saying. I *want* to marry you."

"You're just saying that because of Justice, because we got so emotional over his disappearance. We can just date. You can live here. We don't have to marry to be a family."

He took her hand, squeezed it. "My wanting to marry you has nothing to do with the stunt our son pulled today. I asked Vann for your hand in marriage yesterday, Brielle."

Her jaw dropped. "You what?"

"You heard me."

"What did he say?"

Ross gave a low laugh. "That it was about time and good luck with convincing you to say yes."

A slow quivery smile curved her lips.

"So, tell me, Brielle, how does a man go about convincing the woman he loves that he wants to spend the rest of his life with her, that he wants her last name to be his last name, that he wants her children to be his children, to have his last name?"

Eyes wide and shining brightly, she shrugged. "I imagine he should just ask her and see what she says."

"I suppose if he were smart he'd get down on one knee and do it right, wouldn't he?"

"Or he could just ask."

Putting his hand in his scrub pocket and placing his fingers around the box there, he dropped to one knee and took Brielle's hand.

"Ross, you don't have to do this," she whispered, her voice cracking with emotion. "I'll marry you."

"Shh, haven't you read any fairy-tales? You're not supposed to answer until after I ask."

She bit her lower lip, but was smiling all the same as he continued.

"Brielle Winton, will you do me the honor of being my wife and the mother of my children?"

"I could point out that in all the fairy-tales I've

read the hero didn't ask for the heroine to be the mother of his children five years after the fact."

He gave an exaggerated sigh. "Obviously you've been reading the wrong fairy-tales." He squeezed her hand. "Woman, you are killing me here with your logic when I'm doing my best to be romantic." Grinning, he pulled the box from his pocket, opened the velvet lid, watched her eyes grow huge and fill with tears. "Answer me, Brielle. Marry me and spend the rest of your life letting me love you."

"Yes." She put her hands on his cheeks, stooped and kissed him, his lips, his cheeks, his lips again. "Oh, yes, Ross. I will marry you. I want to marry you. If you're sure."

"I'm sure." His heart swelling so full that he half expected it to burst, he kissed her back. "I love you, Brielle."

"I love you, too. So much. I always have, you know."

"I know." He did know. Deep down he'd always known they belonged together, even when he'd been too stubborn and foolish to admit how much he needed her. "And you always will, Brielle, because I will spend the rest of my life giving you a million reasons to keep on loving me."

"Am I dreaming?" she asked several minutes later when they came up for air, their bodies sated, Brielle's finger sporting a huge diamond that marked her as Ross's woman for all time.

He shook his head. "Nope, this is reality. Our reality."

"Funny," she mused, snuggling closer to him. "It feels like a dream."

"Like I told you earlier, you've been reading the wrong fairy-tales."

"Hmm?"

"Never mind, I don't want you reading fairy-tales," he corrected himself, lacing his fingers with hers. "I want you living a fairy tale, one of our very own with the most amazing, passionate, love story ever."

She rolled over, stared down into his eyes. "I like the sound of that."

"Me, too." He kissed her, then grinned up at her. "I also like the sound of knocking at the front door because that means Vann is here with our son."

Brielle sat up, scrambled to quickly put her clothes back on, then paused to smile at him with love shining brightly in her eyes. "Let's go and tell him a very special fairy-tale, Ross. One where everyone lives happily ever after."

EPILOGUE

JUSTICE LEANED FORWARD and blew out the candles on his birthday cake. Six candles altogether, five for his current age and one to grow on.

Around him, his parents, his Uncle Vann and Samantha, and several of his preschool friends with their parents watched as all six candles flickered.

Had someone asked him what he wanted for his birthday a few months before, he'd have said a daddy, but he had one of those now.

A good one who made his mommy smile a lot. Justice liked that. He also liked all the presents that his daddy was always bringing home for both him and his mommy. Sometimes he didn't understand their giggles, but adults were like that sometimes. Kind of weird and not always as smart as they should be.

After all, he'd been the one to have to go to bring his daddy home. Something his parents had scolded him severely for. How was he supposed to have known that his daddy had already come home and wouldn't be leaving ever again?

Despite the fact that he'd been grounded from the computer—and it wasn't as if he was going to arrange for a taxi pickup at his school again anyway—and hadn't been allowed to play video games for a whole week, Justice didn't mind since he now had his daddy and mommy all the time.

Only they were so busy looking all googly-eyed at each other and kissing each other that sometimes a kid just needed someone his own size to commiserate with.

He blew a bit harder, pushing every last bit of air out of his lungs, watching the last candle go out and made his wish.

He grinned, rubbed his hands together, and looked up at his parents, and couldn't wait for his wish to come true.

Wonder if he'd have a brother or a sister?

He hoped for a brother, but a sister would be okay, too. Maybe.

"What did you wish for, son?" his daddy asked, his arm around his mom's waist as it usually was.

Justice rolled his eyes at his parents. Didn't they know anything? "I can't tell you or it won't come true, but that's okay, because you will find out anyway when the stork shows up."

"The stork?" Ross and Brielle asked at the same time, eyes wide, then looked at each other and smiled as his hand slid around to cup her belly.

Justice wrinkled his nose at the goofy way they were looking at each other and smiling.

His Uncle Vann and Samantha's gazes went to his mom's belly, their mouths dropping open as his mom just smiled and nodded.

Adults. They were so weird.

Justice dipped his finger in his cake, came up with a big dollop of icing, and stuck it in his mouth.

"Mmmmm," he said, grinning as a camera

flash went off, then another. "Is it time for presents yet?"

Because he really couldn't wait to find out if storks made same day deliveries.

* * * * *